TAKEN

ALIEN COMMANDER'S CAPTIVE

HATTIE JACKS

Copyright © 2021 by Hattie Jacks

All rights reserved.

No part of this book may be reproduced in any form or by any electronic or mechanical means, including information storage and retrieval systems, without written permission from the author, except for the use of brief quotations in a book review.

Cover Design: Kasmit Covers

Editing: Epona Author Solutions

❦ Created with Vellum

1

JAYNE

The door to my cell slides open. Every inch of me hurts, and I'm way past caring what happens anymore. I curl into a ball, anticipating a kick in the abdomen. If I don't react, maybe this time they'll leave me alone before they drop the gray blocks that pass as food on the floor.

"Get back!" The guard growls at me. "In the corner! Bow your head!"

He's new. Bigger and angrier than the other aliens I'd seen since I'd awakened in this small metal room on yet another spaceship. Two electric blue markings flash across the iridescent gray skin of his face, marking him as different from the rest of his species. An alien face that twists into a snarl when I don't comply quick enough.

I've been in this strange place for a couple of days. It'd been the first place I'd stayed long enough for the narcotics my previous alien captors had delighted in dosing me with to leave my system and let me recover my wits. My current cell is an improvement on the cages I can recall from the last few months since they abducted me from my wild camping site near my home in England. It might be clean and fresh but it's still a cell and I'm still a prisoner.

My face aches with the beating I took before I arrived on this ship.

On one of the rare occasions I'd been sober enough to speak, I had made some smart remark or other that had landed me in trouble. There is also a nasty grating in my ribs on both sides which makes it hard to breathe.

My new guard draws out a long white tube. I've been around aliens of all shapes and sizes long enough to know that it will cause immense pain if he applied it to me. He flicks at the switch on the tube that I know is a precursor to the painful beam of light that will scorch my skin and yet leave no mark.

I scoot to the back of the cell on my arse as quickly as I can, despite the sickening pain that hits me every time I have to move. I've no idea why these aliens make such a show of strength. I'm an unarmed human, tiny in comparison to them.

Yeah, aliens. I can't even believe I'm thinking the word, let alone being subject to another close encounter. My initial terror at my abduction has, over the months, given way to self-preservation. It's easier to comply than fight.

"Further back!" The big and angry alien yells at me.

"Alright, mate, keep your hair on. I'm moving as fast as I can!" I say, panting my way through the pain.

At least this alien has hair.

"I'm not your *mate*." The guard says grumpily as he moves further into the cell, making the tiny place look even smaller.

"It's an expression. An earth expression. And it really doesn't mean what you think it means. Not a chance, *mate*." I mutter.

He lunges forward and grabs me roughly by the arm. My mouth has gotten me into trouble yet again. I hiss in anticipation of the usual harsh handling. His hand is warm against my bare skin as he runs it down my arm and clips something to my wrist, then snatches my other arm. He's handcuffing me. The cuffs shine brightly and weigh nothing. He goes to pull me up and I can't help but cry out as pain spears through me from my injured ribs.

"Are you hurt?" He asks.

His tone is marginally more tender than before. I brush my long, red hair off my face with my bound hands, exposing my bruised face.

"What do you fucking think? Yes, I'm hurt, not that you give a shit." I spit out.

He lets go of me and takes a step back. My pissy attitude seems to affect his demeanor, at least temporarily.

I get my first proper look at him since he entered the cell, all alpha and angry. From the two red dots on the collar of his black uniform, he obviously outranks the other grunts that throw in my food and push me around.

His head is covered by what looks like jet black feathers, swept back until they curl around his neck. His features are, I suppose, handsome for an alien. High cheekbones and a chiseled jaw. His nose is strong and sharp. His gray skin has a beautiful iridescent sheen that highlights his bone structure. His electric blue facial markings run over his forehead and from under his ear, across his full lips and down his neck. He is well over six foot in height and looks like he is well muscled under the heavy uniform he wears. He is seriously imposing.

The alien male stares at me with piercing orange eyes, looking like he is trying to work out what to do with me.

"I'm to take you to the medic." He eventually says, his earlier grumpy attitude returning.

"Oh, deep joy." I sigh.

I can't imagine that is a good thing. More poking and prodding. So far there has been plenty of that from the other aliens I have encountered. Poking in some intimate places, mostly. I try not to remember.

He grabs me again and I lose my balance, stumbling against him, my poor broken ribs meaning I struggle to stand upright for long. He sniffs the air and recoils.

"You need to cleanse first." He curls his lip.

"Well *excuse* me." All of this shit and now the alien is complaining that I smell. "I haven't had much of an opportunity for a bath. What with the whole alien abduction thing."

I go to wave my hand at my surroundings, but it's stuck to the other one with the cuffs and the gesture is lost. The alien stares at me like I have grown another head.

"Come." He says and drags me out of the cell.

He pulls me down a number of similar looking stainless-steel corridors. All well lit and clean, like my cell, I catch sight of other aliens, with the same gray skin, who quickly get out of our way.

"In here." He pushes me through a door. It's another stainless room, not much bigger than the one from which he took me.

"Strip." He commands.

"No way, mate." I reply.

I might be wearing the old baggy X-files t-shirt and shorts I was abducted in and they might be pretty ripe, but I'm not taking them off in front of this alien. Also, I have no underwear on, and he doesn't need to know or see that.

"I already told you-" He starts to say.

"Yes, I know, and I told you that 'mate' is an earth expression. I'm not taking my clothes off while you are here. No way." I interrupt him as I stare hard into his brilliant orange eyes, stubborn and immovable, even if it's likely to result in a sharp backhander.

"You will remove your clothing." He steps closer to me, menacingly.

"Fuck off." I'm not giving in.

There's a line I am not crossing, and that is voluntarily undressing in front of him. I am going to reclaim my dignity inch by inch, even if it kills me. And he probably is.

He holds my gaze with his deep orange eyes for a long minute. To my surprise, he sighs and takes a step to the side. He waves his hand in front of what appears to be a wall. I notice he has four fingers and a thumb, like a human, all tipped with sharp black claws, very unlike a human. Part of the wall slides away.

"You can cleanse in here. Go in, take your garments off and throw them out."

We stare at each other again for what seems like a long time. I suppose it is a concession and I am desperate to get clean. I admit, I am filthy. Streaked in dirt, my own blood and god knows what else. I stink. My hair is matted in places. Overall, it's not a good look.

"Fine!" I hold out my hands to him. He looks at them and back up at me. "You'll need to take these off Einstein or I won't be able to 'strip'." I give him a shit-eating grin.

He touches the middle part of the cuffs whilst snorting out a breath of annoyance that only makes me grin more. The light disappears, and he catches the central part as it drops into his palm. I immediately turn and head into the other room. I can just about hide around the corner to remove my clothes. It feels weird being naked so close to him. Maybe not weird, but a bit naughty perhaps. I throw out my clothes.

"There. Now how do I turn the shower on?" I ask.

"You don't."

The door slides closed, and I am stuck inside. For a heartbeat I panic. Then I remind myself I have just been in a cell. It can't get much worse. Can it?

"Put your feet in the circles and hold your hands in the air." I hear his voice outside.

I comply, expecting water to fall from the ceiling. Nothing. There is a swishing sound at my feet, and I look down to see sparkling crystals spiraling up my legs. I want to move away but my feet are stuck to the floor. The crystals advance up my body quickly. They reach my neck. I take a deep breath and close my eyes. Death by crystal. That's nice.

I release my breath in a big exhale and open my eyes. The same stainless cubical greets me. Not dead then. I am, however, clean. I sniff my arm. It's a fresh salty fragrance and quite pleasant. My long red hair is soft on my shoulders, not a sticky mess. I hear the door slide open behind me and I turn, forgetting my nakedness. He stands there, gaping. I gasp and try my best to cover myself.

"Clothes!" I yell at him. "Now!" His eyes widen in shock at my command, and he quickly hands me something.

I turn away from him and look at what he has given me. It's some sort of catsuit thing.

"My clothes!" I call over my shoulder. "I want *my* clothes."

"They were bad. I have disposed of them." He says, with a hint of an apology in his voice.

My clothes were the last link I had to earth. Their loss slams me like a train. I bend over, trying not to hyperventilate. It hurts my ribs too much. I recover myself when I realize he's probably having a splendid view of my naked bum, and I pull on the catsuit thing.

"What now?" I ask, flicking away tears from my eyes.

He motions to my hands. I hold them out and I am re-cuffed.

"Medic."

"Oh, deep joy."

2

REX

The silly creature has no idea how the cleanser works and, as a result, I'm treated to a full view of her without her coverings when she appears fully cleansed. The long strands of her hair shining like the flames of the Haaluxian second sun and the gorgeous creamy orbs of her breasts tipped with pert dark pink nipples.

She's a mouthy little thing, referring to me as her mate on several occasions in her strangely accented Haalux, the product of her poor-quality translation chip download, despite me making it very clear that I was not interested in a dirty alien female prisoner, not at all.

As I'm the new Commander onboard *Excelsior*, my orders are that I'm to see to our new captive. A job that is so far beneath me, it's clearly a demotion.

The Captain was on a rest cycle when I made the decision to check out the trade vessel that was trying to sneak through our quadrant. I thought it worked out well for us, given what we found in their hold. The Captain must not think so. He's hardly looked me in the eye since she was brought on board.

I was confident I was in line for second in command of the latest and best battle-class ship of the Haalux Empire. Now I'm not so sure.

It would have been a good promotion and finding her has damaged my chances.

I curse her and my luck under my breath. She's obviously trouble. When I brought her on board, she was out of it. Making a terrible racket, high on illegal narcotics and thoroughly enjoying herself. Disgraceful behavior from a female of any species. The medic, although curious, wanted nothing to do with her in that state, preferring that she was held in isolation until whatever she had ingested had left her system. I didn't want to risk him rejecting her for her dirty state either.

Cleansed and smelling quite delicious, the female says she's hurt, but I'm not going to take any chances, so once she's dressed, I bind her again and she shuffles alongside me, wheezing, as I take her to the med bay.

"Is your face always that color?" I ask as I steer her towards the medical suite.

It's strange, mottled blue, purple, yellow and green on one side. The other side is pink and occasionally flushes a deeper pink, like when I saw her without her coverings. The two halves do not match. One side looks swollen. The strange color of her skin does not detract from her piercingly blue eyes. They are like two *bilik* jewels. Stunning and completely alien to me as I wonder what species she is. She has referred to something called 'Earth' as if I should know what she means.

"It does when some arsewipe punches me in the head repeatedly." She says, her voice sounding bitter. I look at her in confusion. Her sentence does not make any sense. "My face is bruised, damaged." She adds, her eyes blazing at me. "Not that I recall much about who did it to me, given that I was as high as a kite on what they forced into me."

She is referring to the illegal narcotics. Despite what she has done, there is no excuse for torture of any kind by her previous captors. I feel a tinge of relief that she apparently did not take the narcotics willingly.

We reach the med bay, and I push her in front of me.

"Commander Rexitor, what an honor!" Medic Jaal exclaims in delight. "And you're here with our prisoner!" He claps his hands. "I've been looking forward to this! Put her over there." He points to one of the med-pods.

"Why do I get the feeling that this is not a good thing?" She mutters under her breath as I take her over to the pod.

"Medic Jaal just wants to examine you. He won't hurt you." I explain.

I have no idea why I am reassuring her. It can't be because I have seen her unclothed. My Zycle is not due for some time, so I should not be feeling like this about any female, let alone one as tiny, pink and alien as her. I pull myself up to my full height and square my shoulders.

"I will remain here. Do not try anything or you will regret it." I order.

"Give me strength." She rolls her eyes, clearly unimpressed.

"Hop on!" Medic Jaal says to her, patting the pod like he is trying to entice a pet *filix*.

She snorts out a breath of what appears to be laughter and then gingerly climbs on, her eyes wide, staring around at the various screens that light up as she settles herself.

"What species are you?" Medic Jaal asks her as he fusses around with an hypo-syringe.

"I'm human." She says. Her startlingly blue eyes remain huge.

"I thought so! I've never been privileged to have examined one. This is going to be such a treat!" He chuckles.

She shoots him a terrified look. He presses the hypo-syringe to the top of her arm and with a hiss, empties the contents into her.

"This is something to relax you, human. I hope you don't mind." He says to her. "When dealing with an inferior species it is always advisable to use a relaxant." He offers in my direction.

"Oh, that's good!" She breathes, closing her eyes in pleasure.

Her entire body relaxes into the pod as the narcotic circulates. It is strangely alluring. Jaal has a scanner and is working his way over her, asking questions as he goes. She manages to answer them, occasionally opening her eyes, which seem even bluer than before as her pupils have contracted so much.

"You have an object inside you?" Jaal says, jerking me out of my reverie. He is holding his scanner over her stomach.

"What's that?" Her speech is slurred.

"Inside you, something here?" He presses on her stomach. She wriggles sensually and lets out a soft giggle that goes straight to my cock.

"Iss my coil." She laughs, throwing her head back. She looks wanton, dangerous and sensual, although Jaal does not seem to notice.

"I don't understand, what is it for?" Jaal asks patiently.

"It's for birth control. It's in my womb. It stops pregnancy." She says with remarkable clarity before allowing her head to fall back again, one leg dangling sexily over the edge of the pod.

I dig my claws into my palm. I want to reach into her pink folds that I glimpsed earlier, pull out her 'coil' and immediately impregnate her. The feeling is almost overwhelming. My cock is rock hard, and I am pleased my uniform tunic covers it. What is the matter with me? At this rate I'll be asking Jaal to examine me once he has finished with this luscious female. I take a long deep breath and exhale to get my body back under control.

"Humans do this on purpose? Stop pregnancy occurring?" Jaal asks, fascinated. I am too; I wait for her answer.

"Well, yeah." She answers and promptly passes out.

"How much of that stuff did you give her Jaal?" I grind out. An unconscious prisoner is not what I wanted.

"Less than a quarter of what I would give a Haalux female. She is clearly very susceptible to narcotics." Jaal is engrossed in his scanner.

"Everyone who was there when we got her off the freighter knows that, Jaal." I say through gritted teeth.

"On this occasion it is perhaps for the best. She has been badly treated by her former captors. Multiple broken bones. She needs time to heal before any further action can be taken." Jaal says.

"Can you not heal her?" I study the unconscious human. Captain Clarin is not going to be pleased at this news.

"I know very little of human anatomy. I am going to have to study her in order to heal her. That will take time. There is nothing obviously life threatening. In the meantime, if you want her fit for what is to come, she needs rest." Jaal says, studying his charts.

I think that he is quite pleased he gets the opportunity to study a human. I open my mouth to say something about his loyalty, then I change my mind. I need Jaal on my side.

"I will take her back to her cell and inform the Captain of this development." I say instead.

"Oh no!" Jaal exclaims. "That will not do. I need her here to be able to study her and treat her. It will do her no good being dragged back and forth."

"For fucks sake, Jaal!" I mutter. "The Captain is not going to like this, not one bit."

3

JAYNE

I'm awake. I feel very light-headed and weak. I'm still in the med bay on a comfortable bed covered with a lovely warm blanket. For a moment I luxuriate in the feeling of being snug and cozy, very different to what I have known for the past few months.

The night I was taken, there has been the most amazing meteor shower. Alone in my campsite in a wild and remote corner of northern England, I'd watched it in awe. It was better than any Guy Fawkes fireworks I'd ever seen, each exploding cluster of space dust brighter than the last.

One meteor had seemed to descend towards me. The rational part of me, the lawyer–the former lawyer—had been adamant it wasn't falling to Earth.

The part of me craving the adventure that had already landed me in more trouble as a litigator than I could have ever imagined had me up and searching for the meteorite, torch in hand.

I found far more than I had bargained for as I crested a hillock and saw the squat, silver spaceship for the first time. Stunned, I had stood there, open-mouthed, like an idiot. The big green alien that had snuck up behind me had no such dumb reaction.

And now, I'm at the mercy of a whole new set of aliens. At least this ship is cleaner and the aliens easier on the eye. The whole place is made of some shiny metal like stainless steel. It looks purposeful, well-made and solid. The air is fresh too, with an almost lemony scent. As I let my eyes wander over my surroundings, I notice that the male guard from earlier is sat at the end of my pod. His strange orange eyes watch me closely.

"Where's the other guy?" I say, my voice faint and hoarse from lack of use. "The one who shot me up with that stuff."

"Medic Jaal is off shift." The alien says, not moving a muscle. "If you want any more narcotics, you will have to wait." He says with a sneer in his voice. What is it with this guy? What have I done to him other than let him see me naked?

Whatever it was Medic Jaal gave me was both calming and pleasant. Much better than anything else I've been given and without the spectacular hangover. It made me say things I wouldn't normally though. I feel myself color up at the memory of what I revealed.

"Nice as it was, I don't enjoy being permanently off my face." I say to his disdainful expression. "It's you lot that keep pumping me full of that shit." I grumble.

"Why do human females take steps to avoid having young?" He asks.

I remember the conversation about my coil. Oh hell, I want the spaceship to suffer an urgent malfunction to cover up my massive embarrassment. Of all the times my mouth has run away with me whilst I've been under the influence of alien drugs, this has to be far and away the worst. I used to be a professional, a master at keeping my emotions hidden, with the ability to make every word count. I could weave a defense out of nothing. A few months into an alien abduction and I'm unable keep even my most personal secrets to myself.

"It's not always the right time to have a child. Some of us don't want children either. I've never wanted them." I gabble out, seemingly unable to stop myself, there must still be a load of that stuff in my system. "Not that it's that likely I would get pregnant, at my age, I'm thirty-eight."

Why the hell did I say that? Particularly why did I feel the need to tell him how old I am? He really stares at me now and as I flush with my discomfort, I realize I'm naked under my blanket, which makes me even hotter, given his close proximity. Again.

"Humans cannot always reproduce?" He queries.

He seems pretty amazed by the concept. I suppose he's probably never met a human before, given that I haven't actually met an alien either. This is officially the longest conversation I have had with one.

"Human women stop being able to reproduce once they get past a certain age. It's also more difficult for us to reproduce the older we get." I try to explain.

He looks thoughtful. This makes me a little sad and I decide to change the subject.

"What species are you?" I ask, with a smile that I reserve for my most reluctant clients.

He looks as if I have just said I would like to eat his first born.

"I am Haalux. The Haalux Empire is the greatest in the Harom galaxy." He says, his voice strong and rather loud. He imparts this information as if it's something everyone should know.

"Oh." I say without enthusiasm, hoping to take the wind out of his sails. It works. He looks uncertain. I guess these aliens are used to being taken seriously.

"It's Rexitor, right? I'm Jayne Marshall."

I go to pull my hand out from under the blanket, but I'm too weak. Probably a good thing, if I did it wrong, he'd get another eyeful, to go with the one he had the other day, or whenever that was.

"Commander Rexitor." He corrects me, sitting up straighter.

"A formal guy eh? Commander Rexitor it is then." I grin at him. "Pleased to meet you, Commander. Where am I?" I'll build up slow to get the information I need.

"You are on the StarCraft *Excelsior*, the Haalux fleet's finest war-class ship." He says, looking inordinately pleased with himself.

I'm starting to wonder how these guys got to be so great. He seems a little dumb to me.

"So, what does the Haalux empire want with little old me?"

"You don't know?" His eyes flash and he grins.

Ah, shit, I've underestimated him.

"You are to stand trial for the murder of Ambassador Roi."

4

REX

I'm disappointed that she doesn't say anything when I put the charge to her. She doesn't even deny it. Anger rises within me. Maybe it's because I feel invested somehow with her. Just because my body reacted when I saw her unclothed and again in the pod whilst Jaal examined her. I wish the Captain had not insisted that I remain her guard while she remained in the med bay.

I stand and walk over to her. Not sure what I am going to say, I just want her to at least acknowledge what she has done. As I take a step towards her pod an alarm begins to sound. The colour in the room changes to red. Two other medics enter at a run.

"What's going on?" I ask, thinking this must be a trick of hers.

"She has ceased to breathe." One of the medics says as the pair of them fuss around her. "You need to get Medic Jaal, he's the only one who will know what to do."

"Call him on the comms then!" I exclaim in frustration. She has gone deathly pale, all of the pink having left her skin. I have limited medical training but that can't be a good thing for human, as it certainly is not for a Haalux.

"Medic Jaal always turns his comms off when he is not on shift."

"By the great Mother!" I shout in despair.

She is fading before my eyes. Whatever she is guilty of, I don't want her to die like this. I set off at a run out of the med bay and towards Jaal's quarters. On reaching them, I pound on the door until he answers.

"What is meant by this intrusion!" He is half dressed and clearly not pleased. "Oh, Commander, it's you!"

"The human, she has stopped breathing! You need to come." I say through ragged breaths of my own.

Jaal swears and grabs his tunic, pulling it on as he runs back towards the med bay and I follow, impressed by his turn of speed. He quickly takes charge. I watch, helpless, as the team of medics work on the human. I wish I could transfer some of my life force to her. I am willing her to live. Every element of my being invested in seeing her blue eyes again.

My communicator chimes. I have been summoned by the Captain. I swing my gaze from my comm to the pale female in the pod.

"She will live, Commander." Jaal tells me and my heart is suddenly lighter than I have ever felt it.

I practically float from the med bay to attend on my superior.

"You wanted to see me, Captain?" I ask as I enter the bridge. At this time in the shift pattern, there is a skeleton crew. None of them look up from their duties.

"Yes, Commander." Captain Clarin rises from his control bank, and he leads the way across the bridge to his ready room.

Once we are inside, he ensures the doors are closed and presses a code into the wall panel. I recognise that he has engaged a full privacy mode for the area, something that is very unusual.

"What we have to discuss is highly sensitive, Rexitor." He says, by way of explanation. He gestures to one of the seats as he throws himself into the other.

Captain Clarin is a highly distinguished, senior Haalux officer. This much is clear in his impressive head crest and in the deep red color of his eyes. I am pleased I am being taken into his confidence. Hopefully, this is a step closer to being appointed second in command. It is also potentially a step closer to a command of my own. I have worked hard to get where I am, to be the best warrior, to overcome the disabilities that flow from my birth and my appearance.

"You are a good officer," Captain Clarin says, "a good warrior. You are highly regarded in the ranks, despite your shortcomings." It is as if he has read my thoughts. I manage not to react, simply holding his gaze with my own. "However, you have acquitted yourself well in battle and I see great things in your future, Rexitor, which is why I am trusting you now."

"I am honored by your confidence, Captain." I bow my head to him.

"You inspire confidence, Rex." He smiles at me, using the familiar term is a mark of his respect, and he settles further into his seat. "It appears that the human prisoner we have on board is the mere tip of a plot against the Empire."

"A plot?" I query. This is clearly concerning.

"Yes. There appears to be efforts being made by an unknown enemy to destabilize the Empire."

I am unable to stop an involuntary growl escaping at the mere thought that anyone would challenge the might of the Haalux.

"Why would any species challenge us?"

"They hope to destroy what we have built in this sector, starting with the murder of the ambassador. I do not need to tell you how important the resources in this quadrant are to us."

"No, sir."

"The trial will have it out." The Captain says with confidence. "In the meantime, we need to ensure that she stays alive and healthy."

"You think that there is a risk to the human?" I am surprised my heart pounds in alarm, almost as hard as when I thought she was going to die earlier.

"The plotters may wish to silence her before justice is seen to be done. I need you to keep a close guard on her at all times." The Captain fixes me with a stare. "I know you consider this a demotion, Rex, but I can tell you that by performing this duty, you will be providing the best of service to the Empire."

"Sir, you know that I would always do my duty to the Empire." I say, striking my fist to my right shoulder, over my heart.

The Captain inclines his head and nods.

"I knew I could count on you, Commander. Where is the human at the moment?"

Fuck. This is going to be a difficult conversation.

5

JAYNE

There it is. The banging hangover. Delightful. I feel slightly sick. My chest hurts more than ever. It looks like I am still in the medical center; although, I have been moved into my own room. At least the bed is still comfortable and warm. I feel weaker than before if that is even possible. I try to move, but it seems there are a load of tubes coming out of my body, which is gross.

The big alien, *Commander* Rexitor, is still here. He has moved his chair closer to me, and it seems that he is asleep. He has taken off his heavy tunic and is in a tight-fitting top which shows off his impressive muscular physique. There is a soft scent of dark spice, which must be coming from him. I feel my clit throb. So inappropriate. But he *is* sexy when he is not looking at me like I'm something he has found on the sole of his shoe.

Or a criminal.

He accused me of murder. I am not a murderer. I know that. I have spent my entire career as a lawyer upholding the law. Alien abduction is not going to suddenly turn me into something I know I am not, even if I have spent the last few months drugged to the eyeballs. The thing is, the way my big alien spoke, it is as if my guilt is already decided. That's not how any trial I have ever been involved in has worked. Innocent until proven guilty is how it should be.

I wonder if there is any chance I can get away whilst he is sleeping. I ask my previously unresponsive limbs to try again. One arm moves, pushing at the blanket covering me.

"You are awake." His deep voice has me looking in his direction, caught in the act.

He has not moved. His hard, muscular frame catches my eye once again. There is something else hard about him, an unmistakable bulge in his trousers. A really, really big bulge.

"I'm thirsty." I say, tearing my eyes from the bulge and looking into his deep orange ones.

He unfolds himself from the chair and walks the few paces to my bed, looming over me with his soft spicy scent.

"Here." He pulls a tube out of the bed and offers it to my mouth.

I let him place it between my lips and suck. It is cool and refreshing water. For a moment I am lost, closing my eyes at the simple pleasure. Then I feel a slight tug on my left nipple. I open my eyes to find Rexitor rolling it between his thick digits. The blanket must have slipped when I moved my arm. His touch is tender, but demanding, and I feel my hips buck involuntarily in response.

"Do all humans have mammary glands like these?"

He uses both hands to cup my ample breasts as he strokes his thumb across both tight peaks. His eyes bright and curious. I let out a soft moan of pleasure.

"Only women, females have breasts—"

I am cut off as he bends his head and takes one sensitive node into his mouth. His tongue, rough and hot, sweeps across it as he sucks insistently. I grab at his head. There is no way I should be letting him do this to me. It's one thing to be abducted, another thing entirely to surrender my body, even if this alien is sexy as hell.

"Delicious," He murmurs on my breast. His tongue pulses. The heat is intense.

An alarm beeps and it is as if what just happened was a dream. I am covered and he stands innocently next to the bed as the medic rushes in.

"Her heart rate spiked!" He says, looking between me and Rexitor.

"She has just awoken. I may have frightened her." Rexitor says.

Dirty alien. He wants to keep his pleasure quiet. I find myself thinking of what he has hidden in those trousers and how much I would like to get my hands on it. Dirty Jayne.

The medic gives my big guard a look that I cannot quite work out.

"I need to examine her, Rex. Please vacate the bay." He says with a warning tone that indicates he is not to be disobeyed.

Rex gives me a brief glance, nods at the medic, then strides away. I feel a strange ache as he leaves. What is the matter with me? I've no interest in big aliens, even if they are built like brick shithouses and have sexy eyes. This must be some sort of Stockholm syndrome kicking in.

"You ceased to breathe for some time, human," The medic, Jaal, is talking to me. "I am afraid I may have damaged you further in trying to revive you." That explains the pain in my chest, more broken ribs.

"I think I might have had a panic attack when he told me I was accused of murder." I feel my heart increase when I say the words out loud. The last thing I remember was the rushing sound of blood in my ears before it all went black.

Jaal, looks down at me and smiles. His face is a kindly, plumper version of Rex's. I think I like him a bit.

"Commander Rex's forte is not subtley. You are accused of a crime, but it is not our way to try an injured prisoner. It will be some time before you are well enough to face Haalux justice." He says gently.

Putting the inevitable off sounds okay to me. Gives me more time to think of an escape plan. Or my defense.

"Would you like something to eat?" Jaal asks. I nod vigorously, my stomach growling in response.

"I could do with some food, something to drink and—"I squirm uncomfortably, "the toilet." I give him a pleading look.

"The toy-let?" He repeats with a confused look on his face.

"I need to urinate." It's getting urgent. Rex's recent activities haven't helped matters.

A look of surprise mixed with horror crossed Jaal's features.

"Can you walk?" He asks.

"I don't think so." I say with some regret. I'm pretty sure my limbs are not going to cooperate. Jaal looks around a little desperately.

"I will carry you." He finally decides. He reaches into the bay and slides his arms under me. The tubes fall away as he lifts me up. "You are light!" He exclaims. "Haalux females are not light." He grins at my puzzled look.

He swiftly carries me to a small cubicle where there is a sanitary facility like the one in my cell. I rapidly use it, letting out a groan of relief as my aching bladder empties.

6

REX

I'm furious at Jaal sending me out of the room in the med bay where my female lies. The Captain insisted the prisoner should be kept separate from any interference while she recovered, and Jaal refuses her return to the cell block.

I do not know what came over me or why I touched her. It was the sight of her perfect round globes and red peaks as her blanket fell away that tipped my lust over the edge. She responded to my touch in such a delightful way. There was no wantonness, only pleasure. I want to give her more pleasure.

I should not be behaving like this. She is my prisoner, and what is more, she is accused of a high crime that has struck a blow at the heart of the Empire. I have seen the footage from the Ambassador's residence. It certainly appears that it is her firing the poisoned dart that killed Roi.

I have to accept that I will lose her. The mere thought grips at my heart in a way I cannot understand. I've never felt like this about a female, any female, before my first Zycle or after. Not that any Haalux female would want me as a mate, a disfigured male like me inspires either pity or disgust.

I am so wrapped up in my thoughts that I start in alarm as Jaal places his hand on my shoulder. I immediately reach for his, twisting it into a painful position. He yelps and I release him.

"Sorry Jaal." I genuinely mean it. I had no reason to react like that.

"It's my own fault for creeping up on the famous Commander Rexitor." Jaal smiles wanly.

"I'm not famous." I mutter, looking away.

"Oh, forgive me. I mistook you for the Haalux warrior who saved a Council member's son from certain death in the slave pits on Lyra." Jaal grins.

I hate being reminded of that mission. I lost my entire team in that rescue, and regardless of what Jaal says, I am no hero. That is why I am on the *Excelsior* sucking up to Captain Clarin, and I loathe myself for it.

I've been trying to prove myself better than my appearance and my lowly birth my entire life, and right now I feel so tired, I could almost give up. Jaal takes my silence for acceptance.

"She's improving. I have given her something to eat. You can return to guard duties, or maybe have something to eat yourself?" Jaal cocks his head at me as I involuntarily shift my gaze back to her room. "You can eat with her if you like?" Jaal says and I give him a sharp look.

"Why would I want to eat with a criminal?" I say haughtily.

"When is your next mating Zycle, Rex?" Jaal ignores my irritable response. I don't like that look of interest that has crept into his eyes.

"I am not due for another five turns, Jaal, not that it is any business of yours. I do not intend to be on the *Excelsior* when it is upon me." I spit out.

"You are right, Rex, it is no business of mine. I just wondered if you knew that finding a mate can bring on the Zycle early?" Jaal raises his eyebrows in a way that can only be suggestive.

I did not know that. My upcoming Zycle will only be my second since I came of age. I manage to repress a shudder. My first Zycle was such a terrible experience that I'm not bothered that my memories of that time are hazy with sedation.

"Really, Jaal? You are full of useless information. I will take my meal in the mess hall and arrange for someone else to take over my duties." With that, I turn and stride out of the med bay.

Once out of sight, I send a communication to one of my subordinates ordering him to take over guard duties as I head to the mess hall. The place is dimly lit and mostly empty and I breathe a sigh of relief. Once I have eaten, I will take a turn in the training arena to work out my frustration, sexual and otherwise.

7

JAYNE

The food that Jaal has given me is considerably better than the gray coloured slabs I was getting thrown at me in my cell. For a start it has color and texture, though the shapes of the items and smells of them are not things I recognize.

I nibble at a green square-shaped thing that tastes fruity, a bit like a cross between an apple and a carrot, when Jaal returns. I'm not sure I am good at reading alien expressions yet, but he looks rather smug.

"The Commander will be out of your way for a while." Jaal smiles at me. "Although he is sending a replacement, so you will need to be on your best behavior."

I study his face, trying to work out if he is being sarcastic. I end up deciding that he is warning me for my own good.

"Do you not like the food?" He asks, noticing I have not eaten very much.

"Oh no, it's good. I'm just not sure what it is."

I nibble at another yellow cube and find it is savory flavored, which isn't quite what I expected.

"The food I have given you is for invalids. Nutritious and easy to digest." He must have seen the look of confusion on my face as he rapidly continues. "It has similar flavors to some Haalux favorite foods. Got to give the warriors what they like! They are big males!"

He grins at me, and then starts to point out what each colored block represents in terms of Haalux food. I decide I like the green block which is supposed to be a type of fruit called a *Juuli* and a meaty-flavored pink block which sounds like it comes from an animal similar to a pig. Jaal chats to me as I eat, and he checks over my tubes which all reattached themselves when he put me back in the bay. At one point another Haalux warrior sticks his head into my room. He looks much younger than Rex, with the single electric blue marking running across his forehead like Jaal. It's less pronounced than those on Rex and Jaal, which I guess is because of his age. He is swiftly dismissed.

Having finished my meal, I snuggle back against the comfortable bed. I feel sleepy and my vision is a little hazy. I wonder if Jaal has slipped me something, again.

"Tell me about the Haalux Empire, Jaal." I ask, a bit like a child asking for a bedtime story.

He smiles at me in a fatherly way, and I would cry if the drugs would let me. I'd have given anything for parents that looked at me like he is now.

"Haalux is in the center of the Harom galaxy. Over the eons we have conquered many worlds around ours and obtained the co-operation of the others." He says, proudly.

"I meant about the people, the Haalux." I say, sleepily. "What are they like?"

"Our warriors are the best and most feared across this universe. But I think you want to know about one warrior in particular?" Jaal laughs.

"One big sexy one." I slur. I am feeling really tired now. Just as my eyelids droop closed, I see Rex stood at the end of my bed.

8

REX

"More narcotics, Jaal. Hasn't she had enough?" I'm clenching my fists at the sight of my female slipping into unconsciousness.

My work out in the training arena has done nothing to alleviate the dull ache at the back of my eyes, the strange sensation in my chest, or my temper. I really have to stop thinking of her as mine.

"I need to study and treat her, Commander. It may be painful. Sedating her is a sensible precaution." Jaal is fussing around her with an instrument I do not recognize. It is long, pointed and sharp.

"She is not for you to experiment on Jaal." I growl as I step closer. "She must be kept intact for the trial. I am tasked with her protection. If you intend to harm her in any way…" I leave the threat hanging in the air between us, my eyes entirely focussed on the instrument he holds.

"Steady there, Commander." Jaal moves very slowly to place the instrument down. "This is simply a probe that I am using to help her heal. But I will not use it now."

"You will heal her. You will not harm her." My voice is strangled with gruffness.

The blood in my veins pounds through my head. I look down at the sleeping human. Her face is almost completely pink, the earlier mottled coloring that she had called a bruise limited to a slight shadow around her eye. Despite appearances with his sharp looking probe, Jaal is helping her and my blood starts to cool. I sink into the chair next to the bed.

"You may continue, Jaal. I will be watching." I make sure the words drip with menace.

Jaal turns to me, medical scanner in hand.

"As you wish, Commander." He bows his head.

I don't remember him ever being that formal with me. I settle into my chair, watching his every movement. It seems right that I should watch over her, and I feel singularly better for being close to her. Jaal spends some time with my human, moving around the bay until he finally seems finished.

"She is doing well. It will still take some time until she is ready for trial, but she will be ready." Jaal says, softly. "She will need all of her strength, such as it is."

I am surprised at the jolt of fear I get at the thought of her appearing before the Council.

"She is strong?" I recall seeing her pink nakedness. She has no claws or muscles to speak of, just acres of creamy skin that is as alluring as it is soft.

"Far from it in body. Unlike Haalux females, she is delicate. Her bones break easily, and her flesh is infinitely damageable." Jaal is warming to his subject, and I don't like the way he is talking about my female. "In spirit, it is a different matter. She has a strong will to live. That is impressive."

He looks down at her and strokes her hair, which elicits a growl from me. Jaal withdraws his hand and gives me a knowing look that I'm not keen on.

"A strange sort of creature to choose to carry out a murder." Jaal says.

"I have seen the footage, Jaal. It is indisputable." I say quietly.

"Is it? It will be a short trial, then, if you are so sure." Jaal walks past me to the med bay. "If not, and you do not want her harmed, you will need to discuss the evidence with your mate."

"She is not my mate, Jaal." I am far less confident of that than I sound.

"Keep telling yourself that, Commander. I am going off shift. Please try not to kill our prisoner this time." Jaal says, a hint of both rebuke and resignation in his voice as he leaves the bay.

I remain in the chair opposite my female. Her face is peaceful whilst she sleeps. The soft scent of her skin and hair reaches me, and I feel comfortable. The most comfortable since I left her. I could watch over her forever.

9

JAYNE

I'm eating some breakfast when Rex struts in. I don't want to admit, even to myself, that I was disappointed when I had awakened and he wasn't sitting in the chair, his orange eyes open and watchful. I've decided I am definitely developing Stockholm syndrome, although why it has only started to affect me when this particular alien is around, I'm not sure. I suppose it could be his movie star handsome face and glowering looks.

As if in response to my thoughts Rex gives me the benefit his best, angry stare then swipes half a dozen of my food blocks.

"Hey!" I wrap my hand around the remainder as he retreats to his chair, chewing on his ill-gotten gains with an expression of triumph. "Those are my favorite!"

Rex licks each of his digits and a thumb with gusto, his gaze not leaving mine. "Mine too." He takes a step towards me and I cram the remainder into my mouth, my cheeks bulging. I hold his stare as I eventually managed to swallow the lot with a big effort.

We're still doing the staring thing when Jaal walks in, breaking the spell.

"Ah, good, you've eaten!" He bustles around me, ignoring Rex as he checks over my tubes.

"I didn't get to eat everything." I say accusingly.

"Never get between a hungry warrior and his favorite food." Jaal snorts. "I thought you had been to the canteen already, Commander?" He shoots a look at Rex I can't quite work out.

"Can't resist a bit of *Juuli* flavored ration block," He says with not a hint of remorse. "How is our prisoner this morning?" He adds, talking over my head to Jaal.

"Not ready for any sort of interrogation," Jaal retorts.

Rex lets out a noise that sounds like frustration.

"Looks like you are in for another interesting day of human watching." I laugh at him.

He unfolds from the chair and stalks over to my pod, looming over both me and Jaal.

"I've got better things to do than watch you sleep and eat." He growls.

"I'm not sure you do," Jaal says, shifting into Rex's eye line. "I believe your orders are to remain here?"

Rex blinks and steps back, his attitude defeated. "Yes, they are." He concedes.

"As we discussed, why not explain how our justice system works to Jayne to while away the time? She's going to need some assistance." Jaal suggests.

Rex's orange eyes return to me as he weighs up his options. Spend all day staring at me in silence or help me out. He growls low in his throat.

"I suppose every prisoner gets the chance to defend themselves." He eventually says.

"Excellent!" Jaal rubs his hands together in a way that suggests he thinks he has done something good. "I'll leave you together."

I watch him leave, not entirely sure I want to be left alone with Rex. His behavior has swung from playful to aggressive and I'm confused. He flings himself back into his chair and puts his boots up on the end of my pod.

"On the basis this is not considered an interrogation, what do you want to know?" He fires at me.

"What is going to happen to me?" I'm trying to keep the tremble out of my voice.

I've never been in trouble before, not criminal trouble anyway. I studied criminal law, but never practiced it. I might have messed my legal life up, and the thought of being accused of a crime on Earth terrifies me. Now I'm facing a charge of murder in an alien world with an alien justice system that seems to be weighted solely in the favour of my accusers. I push down on the rising panic, reminiscent of how I felt when I was a young solicitor doing my first trials. I must approach this coolly, logically. I have to remember my training. I can't let myself get side-tracked by the big, brawny, and handsome alien male who makes certain parts of me tingle with interest.

"There will be a trial. You will be tried before the Council of Three due to the severity of your crime." Rex says, gravely. "We are too far away from Haalux to return for you to appear in person. You will instead be tried via a holo-link."

"How does the trial happen? Do I get a lawyer?" I'm trying not to let my voice weaken, to appear confident. The swan gliding over the pond.

"What is a 'lawyer'?" Rex asks, screwing his mouth around the word, which clearly doesn't translate.

"It's a person that speaks on behalf of the accused, to present their defense and help make their case." I explain. Although, if he doesn't recognize the word, it doesn't bode well. Rex shakes his head, confirming my fears.

"You make your own case. You will be given access to all the evidence." He lowers his head, pinning me with his orange eyes.

"Okay. Okay." I try and slow my heart rate down. It still hurts to breathe, and I can't afford to hyperventilate. "I can do this. I can do this." I mutter to myself.

I've faced worse odds. I've taken on cases everyone had said were unwinnable and won. I was known for it, lauded even. Until that final case anyway. As I'm struggling to get myself back under control, I see that Rex regards me with interest.

"What is the punishment for my crime?" I need to know what I am up against, what I am fighting for.

"Death." Rex intones with a determined finality.

10

REX

I didn't want to tell her, not just yet. Despite what I said to Jaal, I want to get to know this little human female. I just have to be careful. Not only do I not want to be seen influencing her, I also do not want to be accused of being in league with her. The Captain is already watching my every move.

After what Jaal said about her guilt, I have watched the footage of the ambassador's murder over and over again, trying to find something that would exonerate her. I'm not sure what has driven me to do this. She's an inferior species that holds no interest to the Haalux. She's tiny, easily damaged, and unable to defend herself. She is so small, I can't even imagine her carrying offspring to term. And yet, my heart and mind are only stilled when I'm around her, breathing in her soft scent, watching her breasts rise and fall evenly, regularly. The emotions are hugely confusing and in turn, that makes me angry, despite myself.

She glares at me when I pronounce her fate, her eyes flaming like the colour of her hair. Jaal was right; her spirit is undimmed by the prospect of going before the Council of Three. Yet, death is a real prospect. It's not something that I even want to think about, not for my stunning female, fierce even in the face of death.

"Once Jaal has certified you fit for interrogation, you will get access to the evidence. You can prepare your defense at that point." I know I should be reassuring her. The defiance in her blue eyes has turned to fear. "You should get some rest." I add.

I hate her fear. I don't want to see it in her eyes. I just want to watch her sleeping peacefully as I have the past few nights. Then I don't have to think about anything. My head is clear.

"I can't rest, not when I'm having to think about fighting against a legal system I don't understand to save my life. I need time to prepare my defense because I didn't kill anyone." She is trying to sound confident, her jaw set as she speaks the words.

Hearing the change in her voice gives me an idea on how I can assist her without drawing attention to myself unnecessarily. As I leave the med bay, ignoring the odd smile Jaal gives me, I arrange for my relief and head down to the stores section of the ship.

"Forat!" I shout. I don't want to leave my female alone for long and the *Excelsior*'s quartermaster is nowhere in sight. I call out his name again, louder this time.

"For fuck's sake, Rex!" Forat grumbles as he shuffles into view.

He has dispensed with his uniform and is bare chested, wearing only a loose pair of off duty trousers. His single, perfectly formed Hallan chest marking mocks me. I let out a low growl of frustration.

"Why are you out of uniform?"

Forat yawns and scratches himself. "Late night."

I know what he is alluding to. I am well aware of the drinking and gambling that takes place on the ship, even if the Captain turns a blind eye. It's not something I participate in. I stopped being good company a long time ago and have no desire to associate with others anymore. Anyway, Forat is the closest Haalux on the ship I have to a friend. He might be a complete slob with no regard to protocol, but if I'm in a fight, I want him by my side.

"I need a quality translator-chip upgrade. The full works." I tap my foot in frustration as he blinks stupidly at me.

"You've already got the latest upgrade." He says with a further yawn.

"It's not for me, it's for-" I hesitate. "My prisoner." I should have sounded more confident. Forat is taking an interest.

"Your prisoner? Since when did prisoners get translation upgrades?" He inclines his head and folds his arms. I'm going to have to come up with an excuse or he'll want the full story, and I don't even know what that is myself at the moment.

"Ones that are going in front of the Council of Three need a quality translation chip."

"Oh, that prisoner." Forat says, nodding knowingly.

"What do you know about her?" I snap out and immediately regret it. Forat's head crest flares and I have his attention, whether I like it or not.

"That it's a female, of a pre-spaceflight species, unusual in this galaxy, unless trafficked." He says, inspecting his claws, obviously hoping I'm going to react again.

"Have you got the upgrade or not?" I'm not playing this game any longer. Forat lets out a sigh, stares at me for several long seconds then shuffles off.

He returns a short time later with the upgrade card and hands it to me. I take it but he doesn't let go.

"I am going to need the full story." His voice is soft and insistent.

"I don't have time, Forat. I have my duties to attend to." I know he genuinely cares about me and I would tell him, if I had a story to tell.

"Okay," He lets go of the card, "you owe me, and you know I always get my debts paid." He grins insolently at me.

"Fuck off, put some clothes on and do some work!" I bark at him.

Forat immediately jumps into a Fleet salute, one arm over his chest, his chin tilted high and his Hallan facial marking flashes. "Yes, Commander!"

His tone is suitably mocking, and I'm sure that, as I leave, I can hear him laughing.

Back in the med bay, I dismiss my subordinate. Despite what she said earlier, Jayne is asleep. I indulge my obsession and standing at the head of her pod, I watch her for a while. She shifts and whimpers, her eyelids flickering until they spring open, her blue eyes staring in horror at nothing.

"You are safe." I whisper.

Her eyes find me and focus. She shakes her head. I want to roar in anger that she doesn't believe me. Then reality sets in. I am her captor, why should she believe me?

"I have something for you." I hold up chip tool I procured from Jaal and I check to make sure the download is pre-programmed.

"What are you doing?" She tries to sit up and move away from me as I lean over her.

"Keep still. This will not hurt."

I pull her long soft, red hair away from her neck so I can get to where her translation chip has been inserted behind her ear, as Jaal told me. My fingers lightly brush her skin. It's soft and warm and the crackle of static that flows between us catches me unawares. I hold the tool over the tiny scar and it chimes to let me know it has found her chip. A further chime tells me the download is complete. I pull the long strands of her hair back into place.

"What was that?" She asks, her accent has improved straight away. I don't think I've ever heard a species take to an upgrade so quickly.

"I have upgraded your translation chip. It will assist you with the interrogation and trial. You should also be able to read and write the Haalux language."

"Oh," She dips her head away from me, hiding her gorgeous eyes for an instant. Then their full brilliance is fixed on my face. "Thank you." She whispers and her lips are pressed against mine.

Their pillowy softness is exquisite on my rogue Hallan marking. I've managed to keep control of myself since I touched her last, but her lips on mine strip away my reserve and I'm not sure I can hold back.

11

JAYNE

I hear Rex's voice, smooth and strong in my ears as soon as the upgrade takes effect. The difference is unbelievable, and I forget myself with him. His face is so close to mine I find myself pressing my lips to his in a silent thank you. His mouth is sweet and warm. Warmer over the electric blue skin that flashes across his lips. Skin that heats further at my touch, tingling against my mouth. It makes me want more. I slid in my tongue and entwine it with his.

I'm lost in our kiss, my hand in his black feather hair. It's soft and hard at the same time, the feathers shifting over my fingers. He cups my breast and I immediately want more. I want what he did to me last time and I want him inside me. His kind act was an oasis but that's not what has me kissing him. When he is with me I feel safe and wanted. Not something I have ever felt before.

I had always put my career first. Any relationships I had were fleeting, trampled under my desire to get ahead. Previous boyfriends called me cold and unfeeling, and they were probably right. They didn't matter as much as being a lawyer did. I don't know what I am feeling about Rex, but I've certainly never kissed anyone to thank them before. I guess that the situation has got to me, eroding my carefully crafted control.

He pulls away from me, his eyes closed as his tongue licks the last of my taste from his amazing, heated lips.

"We should not have done that." His orange gaze is strong, and I am confused. I'm pretty sure he was enjoying that kiss as much as I was.

"Whatever," I mutter, smoothing out the blanket that covers me.

At least Jaal has given me clothing again, even if it is one of the figure hugging catsuit things. That was probably the only thing stopping Rex's hands from roving. He couldn't have me there and then, so I'm not worth the bother. His mood swings are making my head ache. I have a defense to prepare, and his behavior has reminded me of the exact reason I didn't bother with relationships. Fortunately, the tension is broken by Jaal bustling in with an air of agitation.

"The Captain has informed me that, whether my patient is ready or not, she is to go for interrogation." He shoots a glance at Rex, who glowers menacingly.

"Who is the interrogator?" Rex's voice is such a low growl I can barely make out what he is saying, even with my new download.

"It's Dagar," I'm not sure I've seen Jaal look concerned before.

Rex lets out a snort and I see a flash of blue streaking over his features, but he says nothing. Jaal turns to me, his red eyes checking me over.

"I'm sorry, Jayne, I tried to hold them off as long as I could. I've insisted that you are returned to me at the end of each session. I also need you to wear this." He winds a black strap around my wrist. "It will monitor your vital signs. If there are any issues, Commander Rexitor will be notified." He hands a small black square to Rex, who snatches it from him. "I have managed to secure the Captain's agreement that if your vitals show you are distressed, the interrogation will be ended."

This remark is aimed at Rex. His face is like thunder; although, he eventually gives a curt nod to acknowledge Jaal.

"We need to go." Rex says, gruffly.

Jaal fusses around me, ensuring that all the weird tubes that are attached to various parts of me are removed. He helps me out of my pod, and I stand on wobbly legs. Jaal wraps a soft blanket around my shoulders.

"Good luck." He takes hold of one of my hands and squeezes it to the sound of another low growl from Rex.

"Let's go!" He says out loud, ushering me out of my room and through the med bay. The eyes of other Haalux males track us as Rex marches through the ship. I try to keep up as best I can, though I'm wheezing by the time he comes to a sudden halt. I nearly run into the back of him.

"Who is this Dagar?" I try to recover my breath, "What do I need to know about him?"

"He is well known as being an effective interrogator. He has some - questionable - methods." Rex says through gritted teeth.

"Oh great!" I pull the blanket tighter around my shoulders. I'm going to be interrogated by the alien equivalent of the Spanish Inquisition, only not the funny one from Monty Python.

"He is not that intelligent." Rex adds as an aside and he presses his hand against a polished area next to the door which slides open.

Rex steers me in through the opening. Sat at a stainless-steel looking table is another large Haalux. He has a single facial marking across his forehead, like the others and unlike Rex. He unfolds himself from the chair and I note with interest that he is at least half a head shorter than Rex, and nowhere near as broad.

"The prisoner arrives, finally." He sneers at me and shoots a vicious glance at Rex.

"You do not need to stay, Commander." He spits out Rex's title. "Your services as a nursemaid are not needed here."

"It has been agreed with the Captain that the prisoner's health should remain monitored throughout the interrogation," Rex holds up the strange black square. "I am to stay."

Dagar looks very put out. It is clear he is oscillating about whether to challenge Rex, who stands behind me as an oddly comforting presence.

"Very well," Dagar decides. "Sit there, human." He barks at me.

I slide onto a hard metal stool. I can feel the cold metal through my thin catsuit. Shivering, I draw the blanket around me more. Dagar stares at me.

"You're an ugly little thing, aren't you? All pink." He says in a low disgusted voice, leaning over the table towards me.

"Can we just get on with this? I'm not in the mood to trade insults." I say, trying to make my voice sound stronger than I feel. I swear I hear Rex snigger. If Dagar heard it, he pretends not to notice. He sits back in his seat, some of the wind taken out of his sails.

"Watch this, female." He presses on a hidden panel below the table and a screen appears as if imbedded in the metal top.

There is footage from what appears to be some sort of security camera. For all the alien tech I have come across, it's not very good quality, at least not to start. It seems to be of a long corridor, flanked by large columns made out of some sort of stone. A group of Haalux males walk past the camera slowly, deep in conversation. A short time later, a hooded figure appears, creeping around the columns. The figure comes to a halt at the column closest to the camera. It pulls out a long tube. As the males walk back into view, the tube fires out something and one of the Haalux falls to the floor. The figure turns to flee, the hood falling back.

And I see myself.

Dagar stops the footage. "That is you, is it not?"

"Well, yes-" I can't deny I've just seen my own face on the screen.

"So, you admit you killed the ambassador?" He grins, exposing long yellowing canines.

"No, I do not! Of course, I don't! Why would I do that? Where is your proof?" I fire at him.

The camera can lie. I know that, maybe he doesn't. From the confused look that flickers over his face, it appears that it hasn't occurred to him.

"Did you really think you could show me that-" I prod the table dramatically, "and I'd just confess?" I may as well rub his nose in it. "I was told I would be shown the evidence against me when I was brought for interrogation. So, show me the evidence!" I end, raising my voice and looking around the room.

Dagar is on his feet, leaning over the table, hot, foul breath into my face. "If you want evidence, we have it, pathetic human!"

His movement is so quick, I fling myself back and fall off the stool, jarring my sore ribs and causing me to let out a cry of pain. He is over the table and has his hands around my waist, pulling me back up, crushing me. I howl at the rough handling, which stops abruptly.

Rex is towering over Dagar. He holds the black square.

"I believe that this interrogation has gone far enough for the prisoner's health, Dagar."

The two males face off against each other. Rex is inordinately calm, Dagar not so much. Eventually he drops his gaze from Rex.

"You can address me by my proper rank." Dagar snarls, although it is clear he has lost this round with Rex.

"As you wish, *Commander*," Rex manages to make the word sound like an insult, and I need to ask him how he does that. "I will return her to the med bay, as instructed by the Captain. You will have the evidence transferred there for her perusal."

At the mention of the Captain, Dagar seems to get his second wind. He moves closer to Rex until they are nearly touching.

"You are not Clarin's pet, Rexitor, not by any means. The Captain won't protect you forever, you freak." He hisses.

Frankly, I'm impressed at Rex's cool under such provocation. I let out a low groan and clutch at my ribs. Dagar gives me a slightly fearful look.

"Whatever," Rex says, parroting my earlier sentiment, "I need to return the prisoner to the med bay to ensure that she is not damaged." He helps me to my feet and tucks the blanket around me.

Without a further look at Dagar, he ushers me out of the room.

12

REX

My female has even more fire than the color of her hair suggests. I had to bite my tongue so hard I thought I would draw blood when she started in on Dagar. The only tool he had left was intimidation, but even then she wasn't frightened. She saw through him straight away. I only stepped in because there was no way I was going to let him hurt her.

"Thank you for helping me out back there." She struggles along beside me and I slow my pace.

"It was my pleasure." I say before I remember where we are and I check the area for other warriors who might overhear us.

"I get the distinct impression that you know that Dagar well."

"Not well, but I know him, yes."

"Why did he call you a freak?" She is looking up at me with those stunning blue eyes that I could lose myself in time and time again. I have to snap out of whatever it is that is causing me to feel this way, and I dig my claws into the palm of my hand, hoping the pain will bring me to my senses. It doesn't. If anything, her scent grows in my nostrils instead.

"He means my extra Hallan," I touch my fingers to my second facial marking.

"I don't understand? I think your markings, your Hallan, are handsome." Her face is open and honest, a sweet smile playing over her lips as she trails her eyes over me.

"I am considered a freak because I have multiple Hallan markings. That is what Dagar meant." I run my hand over my face, to indicate what I mean. He was also referring to my birth, but she doesn't need to know.

"Oh," She appears to contemplate my answer, "I don't care. I like that you have more than one Hallan." She concludes.

I have to battle every atom in my body not to pull her off her feet and have her soft lips pressed against mine again. The sensitive skin of my Hallan at the mercy of her touch. I can imagine her sweeping her tongue over the rest of me.

"You did well with Dagar," I change the subject. "I think you've got him a little worried."

"I know you think I did it, but I really didn't. I would know if I murdered someone. I'd feel it in here." She holds her hand over her breast. "I just need time to prove it, to be able to put forward a proper defense."

"The way you talk, it's as if you have done this before." I take hold of her arm and feel her life coursing through her.

"I haven't!" She exclaims, turning towards me. "I mean, I haven't defended myself against a charge of murder that is. I am - I was - a lawyer on Earth. I have brought and defended many claims for other people, my clients. It is how most human civilizations handle their justice."

"Haalux are expected to be able to defend themselves, in the fighting arena and in the justice system." I explain.

"Don't you have crime or disputes between parties that need representation and mediation on Haalux?" She asks, earnestly, clearly warming to her subject.

"Disputes are settled in the fight ring, warrior to warrior." I draw myself up to my full height. "There is little crime on Haalux. Most justice is meted out on the spot." Jayne's eyes widen as she gets my meaning. "Our society is clearly more sophisticated than that of humans if you have such a problem with crime."

A secret smile steals over her features. "I think you're right, Commander. My species is most backwards." She places both hands on my chest, looking up into my eyes, her breasts heaving. "Maybe you could help me?"

She must have seen me twist my mouth because she hurries on. "I don't mean with the evidence or anything. I don't want you to get in trouble, but perhaps you could tell me more about how your justice system works, as a trial is clearly unusual, so I can prepare my case properly. You know, things like how I address the Council, how the proceedings will run, stuff like that?"

Despite me telling her that her species is primitive, her intelligence is incredible. She has immediately turned her weakness into an advantage, cleverly giving me a way of helping her without appearing to help her.

All I want to do as I stare into her stunning blue eyes is toss her into my arms and carry her to the docking bay. I could put her in a shuttle and in a heartbeat we would be away from the *Excelsior,* and I could have her all to myself. The thought of her lips on mine, of my cock sheathed in her as we move as one. My seed flowing into her as our bodies entwine causes my body to react, my shaft stiffening.

"Please, Commander? I know you think I'm guilty..." She tails off at my silence and I'm jerked out of my dirty reverie.

"I will help you, and you can call me Rex."

My attraction to this female is going to cost me; I know it. Maybe I can make a case to the Captain that won't make me look like I'm collaborating with the traitor.

"You know," Jayne's breathing is labored as we reach the med bay, "all this time in space since I was taken, I've never seen the stars."

13

JAYNE

Mr. 'You can call me Rex' alpha alien will help me. Little old criminal me. Aren't I the lucky one?

I saw lust flare in his eyes just before he agreed, and it sent an answering heat through to my core. I wonder if I'm prepared to pay the price of his help. Not that I can shake the fact that I do find the big guy sexy, incredibly sexy in a smoldering, scary, gruff way.

When he suggested that his gorgeous electric blue markings were somehow wrong and marked him out, I was stunned. He's got the face of a Greek god and the bone structure to match. I would have thought there is no way anyone could find him anything other than devilishly handsome, but it sounds like I'm mistaken. That makes my heart feel funny, almost as if I care for the grumpy bastard.

Although the other reason for my heart feeling odd could be my struggle to breathe. I think that twat Dagar has done some further damage in his rough handling, even though Rex stepped in when he did. My ribs ache, and I stumble a little as we get back to the med bay.

"You were supposed to be taking care of her!" Jaal exclaims as soon as he sees me.

I'm scooped up in his arms and spirited through to my room. Rex is hot on his heels. I can hear his growl of discontent behind us. Jaal deposits me on the bed and starts to reattach the tubes. I immediately feel the benefit. He places a plate of coloured blocks on my lap and urges me to eat.

Once I'm settled with a meal, Jaal leaves us alone. As he walks past Rex, he gives him the evilest of looks. Rex has the good grace to look embarrassed as he stands at the end of my pod. I pick at my dinner, trying to avoid Rex's solid orange gaze.

"What did you mean earlier when you said you were taken?" He says, his rich, deep voice intruding into my thoughts.

"I meant I was taken from my planet, Earth, against my will." I pop a purple-colored block in my mouth and it explodes across my tongue with the flavor of chocolate. I search my platter for another one, disappointed when there are no more. "Or did you think I somehow signed up to be drugged, abused and accused of murder?"

It's my turn to stare at him for a change. He shifts uncomfortably on his feet and then deposits himself in his chair.

"I don't know what to think," He admits. "All I know is what I have seen."

I snort out a harsh laugh. "Yeah, you and me both, Rex."

"Pre-spaceflight planets are supposed to be off limits by general agreement. Do you know who took you? What species?" He wears a serious expression as if it is his duty to police the Galaxy.

"If I could remember anything, I'd tell you. They were very keen that I spent most of my time drugged to the eyeballs." I finished off the glass of liquid Jaal gave me. It tastes like lemonade. "I also don't want to sound like some backwards 'pre-spaceflight' species," I make the invisible quote marks in the air, "but for a while, an alien looked like an alien to me. The only way I could tell you all apart was the number of limbs."

Rex's face has darkened at my words. "Do you know why you were taken?"

"Wrong place, wrong time, I suppose. Where I live on Earth is a country called England. I was out on my motorcycle," Rex looks confused, "it's a form of Earth transport, on two wheels." His eyes widen further and it appears that misogyny is alive and well in the Harom galaxy. I ignore him and continue. "There was a meteor shower the night I was abducted. I thought I saw a meteor hit the ground, and I decided to go looking for it."

"Were you on your own?" His strange feather hair flares up in a crest.

"Yeah, I was alone. I do a lot of things on my own. I was on holiday, well, a break from work."

Break from work, that's one way to describe being fired and escorted off the premises by security while my whole world crumbled around me. Facing down the disappointment of my parents who only ever cared about my career. Well, they would be doubly disappointed that I chose to run away rather than face the music, given that I have literally disappeared from the face of the earth.

"Why would you go looking for something so dangerous on your own?" Rex sounds incredulous.

"A meteor isn't dangerous." I retort.

"Haalux females would never risk themselves in this way, they take their breeding responsibilities extremely seriously." He replies. I blink at him. He is completely earnest and what I thought was sexism is something entirely different.

"Haalux sounds like a barrel of laughs." I start to giggle. I'm feeling pretty good, despite Dagar's attentions. I have so much to learn about the Haalux.

"So, human, you say you've never seen the stars?" He's mocking me.

"Not from space, idiot. Space flight was reserved for a handful of humans. I've only ever looked up at them from Earth." I giggle again.

I'm feeling floaty and happy. Jaal was rather insistent about my rest so there was probably something in my food that helps me relax. I suspect he thinks he's doing me a favour. Rex seems to have moved fast. He stands next to me all of a sudden, taking the remainder of my food from my limp hands. He's so sexy for an alien. Up close, his electric blue facial markings glow, and I long for the touch of his lips on mine.

From the way he's looking at me, I think I might be saying my thoughts out loud. I cover my mouth with my hand. He gently lifts it away and presses his mouth on mine.

"Rest now, little female." He whispers in my ear, and I can no longer keep my eyes open. His handsome face is the last thing I see.

14

REX

"Captain?" I enter his private quarters. He had agreed to my audience request readily, maybe too readily.

"Commander," He inclines his head, his crest flaring with interest. He indicates I should sit. "Update on the prisoner?"

"She is with Dagar," It took a spectacular effort on my part to leave her with him. I had no choice, not if I want to get the necessary permissions. "He is unlikely to extract a confession." I manage to hide my smile.

"She is tougher than she looks," The Captain looks down at his console, "than her physical condition belies in any event."

"That is what I am told by Medic Jaal."

The Captain sits back in his chair. "You wanted to see me, Commander?"

"I have a request, Sir. It comes from the prisoner, but I advance it because I believe it will assist the Empire."

"Go on." I appear to have piqued his interest.

"She, the prisoner, wants more information on how the trial will take place. She wants to be able to present properly before the Council of Three. I believe it would be sensible that she can see the holo-suite where the trial will take place."

The Captain is silent, contemplating my request. I try not to hold my breath.

"I agree with you. We want the trial to appear fair. She should be seen to be given an opportunity to present herself well. When she fails, then Haalux justice will be seen to be done. But there is nothing to be gained by making her look more primitive than her species already is." He nods his head. "I accept your request, Commander. Please ensure she has what she needs."

I take my leave and try not to appear as if I am in any sort of rush as I stride through the ship, back to the interrogation suite to extract her from Dagar's clutches. Subordinates scatter in my wake. I've clawed my way to my position by sheer force of will and show of strength. Most of them have come up against me in the training arena. They only spar with me voluntarily once.

I walk straight into Dagar's interrogation. If he has mastered his role, my sudden appearance should not concern him. Jayne sits on her stool, looking cool, collected and, this time, unharmed. My sudden entry clearly has bothered Dagar.

"Commander Rexitor, I am not finished here." He spits out.

"I think you are," Jayne says. Her voice is soft, her accent less marked than before. In a few days she will be fluent. "I think we are done here, Commander Rexitor." She looks at me, and there is a twinkle in her eye that I am beginning to recognize, "I'm tired, please check my vitals."

I pull out the recorder that Jaal gave me and make a show of checking it. Jayne is absolutely fine.

"You are showing signs of distress. I am therefore bound to return you to the med bay. If you agree, Commander?"

Dagar grunts. He has failed to interrogate the tiny female. He knows it; the Captain knows it. My heart swells with pride for her. I take Jayne gently by the arm and she gets to her feet, walking in front of me and out of the door without a backward glance.

"Take care, Rexitor," Dagar says in a low voice, "there are forces at work that are far more powerful than you can imagine."

I take no notice. A good opponent knows when he is beaten. Dagar is not a good opponent.

Jayne is already heading down the corridor in the direction of the med bay and I quickly catch her up.

"This way," I press my hand in the small of her back, luxuriating in the warmth that emanates from her.

"Where are we going?" She asks, trotting along side of me. Her breathing is much improved.

"You asked for my help and I am helping." We have reached the holo-suite.

"This is where the trial will take place." I fire up the programme and the suite morphs into the Council chamber.

Jayne jumps and moves closer to me as the chamber reveals itself in all its circular glory. The walls drip with the elongated silver *Yanini* crystals flowing into the floor that flashes with *Nenei* diamonds. The platform upon which the Council of Three sit hovers high above us, their presence suitably obscured. The onyx black tiers for the statutory council members stand empty for the time being.

"You will stand here." I point to the dark red circle, raised slightly from the floor. "You will be unable to move from this spot due to the forcefield around you."

Jayne stares around in awe, her intelligent eyes taking in every detail. "I can have my notes with me though?" A sensible question.

"You may. Also, as the Council will want to see the video evidence, you will be able to control this as you see fit." She's so close, her glorious scent surrounds me. "The Council will sit up there," I point up to the platform. "The Assembly around you. They will be vocal, but the final decision is down to the Council of Three."

Jayne takes in a shuddering breath. "How do I address the Council?" Her entire being is concentrated on the task in front of her—her fight for her life.

"You address them as 'Honored *Tesei*'". I say with a solemnity that I do not feel towards the Council. I might have saved the son of councilor Mejin from almost certain death, but that granted me no leniency towards my own lowly birth and unusual appearance.

"Honored *Tesei*," Jayne mimics me, wrapping her tongue around the unfamiliar word with ease.

"The prosecutor will stand over there," I point to the gray stone plinth. "And the screen for the footage will appear next to him." I explain.

"Who will be presenting the case against me?" She asks, her eyes not leaving the plinth.

"Dagar." I say his name through gritted teeth.

His words from earlier ring in my ears. I've always avoided Haalux politics where I could. It's been hard enough for me to rise to my current position on merit alone without having to battle the invisible web woven by others. To my surprise, Jayne starts to smile. She walks around the holo-suite, inspecting the various elements of the chamber and looks remarkably calm.

"If you have seen enough, we should go." I say to her softly.

"I've seen enough." She replies, her face grim.

15

JAYNE

What Rex showed me might have been a clever trick of light, but every part of that chamber is designed to intimidate, even in holographic form. What's more, it is designed to intimidate the largest of Haalux males. Males like Rex. I feel like a Victorian urchin faced with The Old Bailey.

I am innocent. I feel it in my bones. It doesn't matter that I can't remember what I have done in the last weeks or months since I was taken. I spent my time in the interrogation with Dagar persuading him to rerun the footage as he attempts the worst line of questioning I have ever encountered. Maybe no one told him that continually shouting 'confess' is not a way to get a suspect to confess?

There is something strange about the me on the tape. Rex said I would get access to it, and I'm going to need my own version soon enough.

I had seen enough of the Council chamber by the time Rex suggests we leave; it's imposing crystalline structures burnt into my brain. He ushers me out of the chamber and into the corridor of the ship. It seems bright by comparison and I'm blinking with the change.

"Come with me," Rex starts to lead me in the opposite direction to the med bay.

"Where are we going?" I'm intrigued.

He doesn't seem the type to go off script. Originally, I thought his warrior appearance meant he obeyed orders, however I'm not so sure, not after he got me the translation upgrade. I'm pretty sure prisoners don't usually get that sort of treatment.

"You'll see," He takes me gently by the arm, his touch almost protective, as he leads me through the ship until we finally stop in front of a nondescript stainless steel door. Rex presses his hand against a pad at the side and the door slides open.

It's dark as he guides me inside, and I soon realize why. In front of me are floor to ceiling windows looking out on to the rushing, sparkling stars and emptiness of space. I rush forward, pressing myself against the glass. I really am in space. This is not a dream. I'm at once awed and terrified.

Looking down, we are passing over something that looks like a multi colored cloud filled with diamonds. It swirls and morphs as we pass.

"It's-" I can't find the words as Rex joins me. His bulk and warmth reassures me against the vastness of space.

"I've seen plenty, but the sight of the stars from the stars is always one I respect and honor." He says in his deep voice.

At this moment I am glad of the translator upgrade has allowed me to properly understand the nuances of his words.

"Jewels cut out of a sun." I murmur, and I feel his questioning gaze on me. "Something I heard once," I explain. "I never really understood it until today." I press my hands against the glass, wanting to fall into the velvety blackness, just as long as Rex can fall with me.

I cannot understand my visceral attraction to him. It seems to come from my very center, my core. When I look into his eyes, I can tell he feels it too.

He is very close now. I feel his breath in my hair, and as I turn, he wraps his arms around me in the darkness. With only starlight on his face; his electric blue markings appear to pulse. The draw he has on me is unfathomable. Those full lips are too inviting, and I raise myself up to taste him. The heat of his skin on mine causes me to delve deeper into his mouth, my tongue roving over his sharp canines and entwining with his.

He cups my face in his large hands, his fingers pushing in my hair as he leans into my kiss, pressing me against the glass. I melt into him, molding my body to his. Under his stiff tunic I can feel something hard and big. Really big. I wonder exactly what he is packing down there, how alien it might be, whether it will even fit. I pull away, breathless. Being with him seems so right and yet I know it's not.

"Is there something wrong?" His orange eyes study my face, and for the first time he looks innocent and even a little scared.

"I don't know if we should do this, Rex." And yet I press a kiss on his jaw, causing him to close his eyes in pleasure. "I don't want to get you into trouble."

"I need you, Jayne. More than I've ever needed anything." He whispers. His eyes open wide at his own words, as if he never intended them to be heard.

The thing is I feel the same way. The mere thought of whatever it is he has under that tunic slipping inside me turns my legs to jelly. I sag in his arms, and he captures my lips once again. The heat from his electric blue marking sparkles against my skin, pulsing through to my core, which clenches in anticipation.

"I want you too."

"Not here," He says into my ear as he kisses it softly.

He takes my hand and leads me through the door, through several corridors, thankfully empty until we reach one that is dotted with doors. He enters one, with me following behind him and I find myself in a cabin. It's small, dominated by a large bed, but it has windows to the outside.

"Is this yours?" I ask.

"As a commander I get my own cabin. My subordinates share their quarters."

His hand is on my waist. Whilst he seemed to be in control earlier, now he is hesitant. I wind my arms around his neck. Lifting myself on my toes to nuzzle at him, I draw my hands down and pull gently at his tunic. It parts down the middle, and I quickly pull it off his shoulders, down his arms, freeing him from its starchy confines. Underneath his chest is bare, more jagged electric blue markings circle over his chest like a collar. In the dim light of the cabin, I swear they are lit from within. I trace my fingers over them, and he lets out a low groan. They are hot to the touch, glowing beneath my hands.

His tight trousers clearly show the outline of a member that is much larger than I anticipated earlier. As he captures my mouth in another kiss, I run a finger around the waistband, wanting to know what I am dealing with, what I want more than anything else.

Rex pulls at my catsuit, stripping the stretchy material from my body until he has exposed my breasts. His big hands can easily hold my heavy flesh. He sweeps a thumb over a tight peak and the pleasure spears through me. I push my hand into his trousers and grasp at the biggest cock I have ever had or seen. It is fully erect and almost vibrating with hardness, I can only just get my hand around its girth and I can't even hazard a guess at its length. His hips buck against me as I stroke his shaft, further groans escaping his lips, still pressed against mine. He kicks off his boots even as he pulls at my catsuit, freeing me from its confines. Then he slides out of his trousers. We are fully naked as he picks me up and tosses me onto the bed.

16

REX

I want to take this slow. To enjoy every second of mating with my beautiful Jayne. My body has other ideas. I've never known my cock this hard. It has not stirred since my last Zycle, not once. It aches to be buried in her soft cunt.

I lay her out before me and work my way over her body, denying my cock until I have had the opportunity to pleasure her completely. Starting with her red hard nipples, I suck one into my mouth. She moans and squirms under me in a delicious way that has my cock rigid against my stomach. I turn my attentions to her other nipple, licking and suckling at the delicious bead as I let my hand trail over her stomach and down towards her triangle of soft curls, the only other hair on her body.

I toy with their softness briefly before my fingers slips between her legs and explores her heat. She is wet, very wet. Moisture drips from her and allows me to push two digits inside her. She is incredibly tight, and I wonder if she will even be able to take my cock, small and delicate as she is. I play with the sweet pearl that causes her to moan and squirm. The aroma of her arousal is almost overwhelming as she pushes up against my hand, wanting more and more until she convulses, flooding me with moisture. I withdraw my fingers and lap at them, tasting her, sweet and delectable.

"Are you ready, *kedves*?"

I cannot hold back any longer. The desire to be inside her is overwhelming. Everything about her is perfect, from her blue jewels of eyes, half lidded with pleasure, to her gorgeous body, creamy and delightful.

"Yes!" She groans as I part her thighs, lifting my body over hers, my throbbing cock pushing at her delicate entrance.

She kisses me with hunger, her mouth plundering mine, and I thrust forward, filling her with one swift movement. She takes me completely even as she gasps at my invasion. Her tight, sweet pussy grips me, and I am almost afraid to move.

"Oh, Rex!" Her voice is barely a whisper as she clutches me to her.

I withdraw, slowly, carefully, enjoying every last inch of her soaking channel before I piston back inside, fitting perfectly as she wraps her legs around my waist. I begin to move, my hips circling with each thrust as she moans in pleasure. I lift myself so I'm able to watch her tight pussy milking me, my cock slick with her moisture as I withdraw and return to her warm, wet embrace. Every second inside her brings me closer to my climax, to spilling my seed in her.

I increase my strokes, driving harder, deeper as she clutches at my shoulders, molding to me and urging me on with short sharp cries, her breath in my ear, panting at our movement together. I feel her clamp onto me, sucking at my cock, pulsing and relaxing as her orgasm shudders through her. It tips me over the edge and my cock releases its heavy load. My vision of her wavers as my climax thunders through me. My cock pumps and pumps, filling her tight channel. Blood sings in my ears at the intensity of my orgasm. I have taken my mate; I have claimed her and marked her as mine.

17

JAYNE

I wrap my legs around Rex's slim waist as he slips inside me. His enormous member stretches me to my limit. Not only is he incredibly hard, but his cock seems to be ridged, and I feel every single bump as it penetrates my pussy. It hits my G-spot perfectly. I clutch at his muscular shoulders and gasp in delight. He holds himself inside me for a minute, his orange eyes studying every inch of my face and then he withdraws with aching slowness. Lifting himself up, he exposes us, his cock glistening as he slips it in and out of my tight channel. A long electric blue marking runs the full length. With each thrust, it sparks against me, sending a pulse to my clit. It is as if Haalux males are designed to cause a female maximum pleasure.

I've never been filled in the same way by a human man, not like Rex. With him, the experience is total. I pull him to me as he begins to thrust, hard and fast, just as I like it. His mouth finds mine, and I suck at his tongue and lips, feeling the tingle on my skin from his markings. The heat they give out adds to my heightened arousal. Rex grunts in delight as I shift my mouth from his to nibble at his earlobe. He keeps up the pace he has set; our bodies entwined completely as I feel my climax burst over me. My vision sheets white as my pussy pulses hard and long over his cock, wet and filthy, milking him, needing him to orgasm, too. He follows me into our forbidden pleasure and lets out a low roar as he comes, hard and long inside me, spilling his hot seed in ropes I can feel with a spicy heat. His thrusts become irregular as he lets rip with his orgasm. My body reacts with a further wave that convulses through me, shuddering my sweaty body against his as it tries to take every drop of him.

Rex holds me to him as we finish together. His strong arms encircle me, holding me against his hard muscular body, and he buries his head in my hair. As we recover our breath, I feel the heat draining from his markings. He slowly rolls to the side, still keeping me in his arms, careful not to crush me.

"I should not have done that." He says, blowing out a long breath, his eyes still closed.

I freeze. I thought this was what he wanted, what I wanted. He looks at me and his brow furrows.

"I mean, I should not have been able to do that. I am not due on my Zycle for another five turns." He pulls me closer to him. "I enjoyed it very much, beautiful Jayne." He presses a kiss to my forehead.

"What is your cycle?" I relax a little into him, his spicy scent surrounding me.

"Zycle," He corrects my pronunciation. "Haalux had a population collapse around a hundred turns ago. Our scientists at the time decided that reproduction needed to be more controlled. They made modifications to the genetic makeup of male and female Haalux to ensure healthy reproduction levels."

"That sounds like an extreme response."

"Maybe. What it means for males is that we have a reproductive Zycle once every ten turns. During which we must mate continually for thirty days. For the remainder of the time the urge to mate is reduced or removed. Our females remain in a state of constant fertility." He explains, his voice sounding strained.

"You have to mate for thirty days?" I twist to look up at him. His face has taken on a pained expression.

"If we do not find our fated mate, we have to service willing Haalux females for thirty days. As males in Zycle can be dangerous, we are usually restrained during this period." He closes his eyes.

"You are tied up and made to have sex? And my species is considered to be inferior?" I half-laugh and half-sob. "Has this happened to you, Rex?" I am horrified at the thought of the proud warrior being abused in this way. There is also the nauseous feeling of jealousy there, even though he is not mine to be jealous about.

"I have had one Zycle since I came of age." A shudder rips through his strong body. "I could not mate with any females. I was put on the machine instead."

"Oh, God, what the hell is that?" I say, horrified.

"It milks us of our seed, to be used to impregnate females. It means that a Zycle is not wasted if a male is unable to perform. We remain sedated throughout the process."

I have no words. It sounds brutal and cruel. Instead, I snuggle closer to him.

"So, what's going on now, if you are not in your Zycle?"

"I don't know." He is silent, although his arms curl further around me, pulling me on top of him. "I need to get you back to the med bay, before anyone realizes you are missing." He dips his head to capture my lips in his, "I'm sorry little *kedves*."

He holds me for a bit longer until he shifts from under me and collects my catsuit from the floor. He hands it to me and then pulls his clothing back on. When we are fully dressed, he takes me in his arms again.

"It's going to be okay, Rex," I whisper into his chest.

It's not. I don't know what this is between us, and I'm going to die anyway. Perhaps if I say it enough, one day it will all be okay.

Because that worked out well for me in the past, didn't it?

18

REX

I brought Jayne back to the med bay and reluctantly left her with Jaal whilst I obtained a data-pad that she could use to review the footage and make her 'notes'. When I returned, she was safely tucked up in her pod. I gave her a brief run down on how to operate the device. She picked it up quickly and has been working for a good hour, her face a mask of concentration.

I don't think I have ever met any species that has been able to absorb an upgrade to their translation chip as quickly as Jayne. She is able to read and write our language with ease. I wonder if she is the exception amongst her kind. From what Jaal says, they are a young species, and that's probably why they are pre-spaceflight. I relax in my chair as I watch her working.

Relaxed isn't the word for how I feel. I had no idea that a mating could be as deeply satisfying as the union that Jayne and I shared. The one female I had let anywhere near me during my first Zycle had managed to get me to enter her, but I had rejected her so violently, she was removed. After the third try, I did not recall anything until I woke up on the machine. My remaining days were hazy with pain and sedation. That was why I intended to ensure I'm not on the *Excelsior* for my second Zycle. Jaal has a room full of sedated males in

Zycle on machines. Just the sound of their groans chills me to my core.

It turns out, for once, I am being watched, not doing the watching. Jayne has laid down her device, her knees drawn up to her chest, her blue eyes fixed on me.

"Hey," She says, "you were miles away."

"I was right here," I say, not understanding why she is suggesting I left her. I would never leave her.

"It's an Earth expression," She smiles at me, "It means you were lost in thought."

"I was." I acknowledge.

"Anything I should know about?" She picks at something on the blanket covering her legs.

"No, nothing to worry you." How do I explain to her that I believe she is my mate. She may not even mate in that way. After all humans have 'birth control' which suggests they have multiple partners. I might just be a passing fancy to her.

The trial outcome is guaranteed; she will lose her life. Fated is a concept that can be applied to more than just mates.

"Okay, well, do you want to hear some good news?" She says her blue eyes sparkle with intelligence.

"I most certainly would."

"I think I have a defense." She grins.

"That is good news!" I try to remain upbeat. "How?"

"It's what I do. It just takes a bit of lateral thinking. When does the trial begin?" She pokes at the screen a couple of times.

"It is scheduled for the day after tomorrow, provided Jaal gives you a clean bill of health."

"I think he will, if I ask him." She replies, confidence radiating from her.

"You want to go to trial?" I remember the look on her face in the Council chamber. And the look on her face when we mated. I know which one I want to see again first. My cock twitches alarmingly under my tunic.

"It's what I do best- did best. There's no point prolonging the inevitable." She grins.

I want to leap into the pod and devour her. She is intelligent and fierce. A tiny tendril of hope enters my breast that if anyone might be able to convince the Council of her innocence, she can.

"Rex?" The sound of my name on her lips is music, "Don't you think it's odd that, out of all the known species in your Galaxy, I turn out to be the creature that is set up to murder your best ambassador?"

"I have come across killers of all shapes, sizes and species. There is not a type."

"But that's the point. Out of all the known species. Why choose a primitive, unknown one? If you accept that I did kill your ambassador, either under duress or under the influence, there were surely plenty of much more suitable killers to choose from who would not leave a trail to follow or even a digital imprint. They would have been like smoke, disappearing into the walls. Yet, here's little human me. Caught on camera, then caught by your flagship, off my tits in a cage on a trading vessel. Surely you think that is weird, or at the very least a coincidence too far?" She has warmed to her subject, red spots appearing on her cheeks as she seeks to convince me of her argument.

She has a point. Using a human to kill the ambassador, an unknown species with no specific attributes to killing, does seem farfetched.

"You really have done this before, haven't you?" My female is beautiful and intelligent. A mate I'm not sure I'm worthy of.

She drops her head, her eyes not meeting mine. "I did used to do this. Then I made a mistake. That was the reason I was out in the middle of nowhere. If I had not pushed so hard, maybe I wouldn't be here now."

"I believe you have a chance." I say, my own hope rising. My clever mate has spotted a flaw, a crack in the evidence around her. It might be the difference between me keeping her at my side and losing her and I'm going to take whatever we can get. "I want to help you, in any way I can. Just tell me what you want me to do."

19

JAYNE

Rex has not left my side since we made love. From past experience, I know he should have called in his relief, a younger Haalux warrior who doesn't even look me in the eye. Instead, Rex cleanses in my bathroom and eats beside me. I'm not sure if this is the best move for him, even if he says he wants to help. However, he seems set on the idea.

We work through what will happen at the trial, how it will be structured and what opportunities I will have. I must accept that without him I would struggle. I might know what I am doing in constructing a defense, but not knowing their justice system is like trying to ride my motorcycle blindfolded with my throttle arm tied behind my back.

Eventually, Rex has to attend on his Captain, and reluctantly, he leaves me. Jaal appears in the doorway to my room as I continue to work on my defense.

"You appear to have won over at least one Haalux." He says from his position leaning against the doorframe. He pushes off and starts to check over my tubes, releasing me from most of them.

"And you," I reply, placing my hand on his arm. He stills in his work and the smile that spreads of his face is both benign and sad.

"And me." He pats my hand. "I am sorry I could not delay the trial any longer."

"Couldn't have you looking like a poor medic, could I, Jaal?" I laugh. I know that if it weren't for him, I would have been thrown in front of the Council, dazed and in pain, several days ago. Dagar's grumblings made that pretty clear.

Jaal removes the last tube from my side. "You are something special." He says, contemplatively.

"An interesting specimen?"

That makes him laugh. "I don't believe you are capable of killing, any more than I am." He says suddenly.

"And for that, I thank you. It's what I need to hear, right now." My confidence was already at an all-time low, even before I was abducted by aliens, drugged and fitted up for a murder I did not commit. I look into his dark red eyes.

"Why are your eyes a different color to Rex?" I ask, wanting to take my mind off my impending death.

"Haalux' eye color darkens as we get older. I am many turns older than Commander Rexitor. And wiser." He gives me a cheeky grin that belies any age he claims to have.

"Rex said he is different because he has more-" I try to remember the word, "Hallan markings?" I draw my fingers across my face.

"Rex is different in many ways," Jaal says, sitting down on the edge of the pod. "Our society does not like difference. It is built around order and familiarity. A Haalux warrior strives to be the best, to be part of the whole. To do his best for the Empire. He does as is ordered, in war and in mating. Our females breed for the good of the Empire. Commander Rexitor feels that because of his additional markings, he stands out. As such, he believes that he has always had to be that little bit better in order to fit in and gain the position he is destined for."

"I think they are beautiful." I remember the touch of his lips on mine, the tingle of his electric blue skin.

"Then you are as special as I think you are." Jaal squeezes my arm. "Your mate also had to overcome the misfortune of his birth. He was from a forced mating. Even though there is not supposed to be any hierarchy over and above the Council and Assembly, those warriors born from artificial impregnation or a forced mating are colloquially considered inferior."

"Then why do it?" I'm still struggling to understand the world I have entered into. The more I find out the more it's rigid and confusing.

"The Empire needs warriors. Our breeding Zycle is such we must use every drop of male seed and even then, that is not enough for the Empire's needs."

"Why not just change the Zycle? Allow more natural matings?"

"If only it was that simple, sweet human. Your fertile species would think it so. The Haalux would take more convincing."

There is a small sound in the room, and I see Rex standing at the end of my pod. "It is set," he says. "The trial is to take place tomorrow."

He sits down heavily in his seat across the room, and for an instant I see his troubles descend over him like a cloak. I have not made his life any easier, and it weighs on my heart.

"I have some experiments that require my attention," Jaal says to us both. "Make sure you get some rest, Jayne. I am required to give you the final clean bill of health, but as we have already discussed, I have no alternative." He rises and gives me a curt bow. He inclines his head at Rex as he leaves, the door to my room sliding shut.

"You were enquiring about my birth?" Rex says, his voice gruff.

"Jaal volunteered the information," I pick up my data pad, starting to work through my defense. "For the record, I don't pay any attention to stuff like that. Where you came from is simply a starting point, it's what you do with your life that counts."

The harsh laugh that Rex utters has me looking up from my work.

"Look, Rex, you're looking at a woman, a female, who had it all and lost it. My birth had nothing to do with that, I did it to myself. I both built my empire and smashed it. No one else was to blame." I go back to my pad. When I look up again, he looms over me, an unreadable expression on his face.

"You are the most intelligent creature I have come across in a long while. You are prepared to entertain all possibilities. Your mind sees things others do not. Why do you have no belief in yourself?" He asks.

I set aside the data pad and look into his orange eyes, taking in the flashes of blue streaking across his handsome face.

"I took on a case. My client was accused of causing an accident in a factory he owned. He showed me evidence that exonerated him. I believed it and I trusted him. I was wrong. My cross examination of his victim resulted in the poor man trying to commit suicide." My breath catches in my throat at the memory. "My client lied to me and a man died. And when I lost the case, he destroyed me. I lost my job, my career, everything." I dip my head.

The shame overtakes me, tears falling even as I scrub at my face. These are nothing compared to what I put my client's victim through. I pride myself in my self-control, but the memory of my failure is overwhelming.

I feel Rex's hand in my hair. "How can a lie told to you be your fault?" He asks gently

"I was an experienced litigator, and I should have known."

Rex cups his hand around my chin and lifts my head so that I am looking at him.

"No one knows everything, sweet female." He uses his thumb to wipe away the tears.

"Even you?" I let out a wet laugh.

"I am the exception." He says gravely. Then he smiles, exposing his elongated canines. I've never seen him smile. His face lights up, and he looks completely different. I find myself wanting to ensure that he always looks that happy, to clear his face of the semi-permanent scowl he wears.

An alarm sounds, high pitched and pulsing. I immediately cover my ears. Rex races over to the door, almost bumping into it when it doesn't open automatically. He presses on a shiny black rectangle at head height.

"Jaal! What is going on?" He barks at the wall.

"My apologies Commander, there has been a release of a dangerous pathogen in the med bay and I have had to evacuate. You have been sealed in for your safety." Jaal's voice comes over some sort of speaker.

"For how long, Jaal? Jayne has to attend the trial tomorrow." Rex grinds out.

"It will take several hours to decontaminate the bay, however, it will not impact on the trial timetable." Even over the speaker, there is a hint of something in Jaal's voice that sounds mischievous. "The door is sealed until the cleaning process has completed. I am afraid you are stuck in there for a while, Commander."

Rex rests his head on the door.

"What are we going to do, in here, on our own, for all that time?" I stare at my big alien captor, allowing a smile to play over my lips.

20

REX

"What are we going to do, in here, on our own, for all that time?" Jayne asks as she levels a heated gaze at me.

She knows Jaal has engineered us being stuck together, where no one can get at us for a few hours. Whether or not he already knows we have mated, I cannot tell, but he wanted us to have this time and my instinct thanks him for it.

I stalk over to where Jayne is propped up in her pod and sink down next to her, pressing my lips to hers, my hand running through the soft, long strands of her hair that glints like fire. She responds readily, her mouth hungrily devouring mine, her tongue exploring, entwining, urgent. She lifts her curvy form to press against me and her hands pull at my tunic, quickly getting it off me. She wraps her arms around my neck and pulls me onto the pod with her, rolling us over until she is resting on my chest.

"Got you where I want you, my warrior." She says, her eyes glittering blue.

She sits astride me and slips her arms out of her garments, her breasts bouncing free. I reach up to caress the tight red peaks, cupping her overflowing flesh in my hands. She leans over me, dangling the sweet treat over my lips, I capture it with my tongue, pulling it into my mouth and suckling hard as she gasps at my touch. I knead at her other breast, lapping at her.

I can feel the heat between her legs over my crotch. My cock is already achingly hard, and her movement only serves to make it harder. I push at her clothing, wanting to reveal her body in all its glory, but she removes my hands and shifts further down my body.

"I want my warrior to enjoy himself." She undoes my trousers, delving in and easily extracting my throbbing cock.

Her tiny hand doesn't even quite encircle it as she pumps me with slow, sensual strokes, before she drops her head and wraps her lips around my cockhead. My hips lift towards her involuntarily, and I let out a groan of pleasure. She laps her tongue over the Hallan marking that runs the length of my cock, and I feel like I am about to come instantly. Her touch is so intense. I place my hand on her head, and she sucks me into her hot mouth, her tongue circling, lapping and exploring my weeping slit. Using her hands and her mouth, she takes me down her throat time and again. I am unable to help myself, thrusting at her, wanting her to take more of me.

She returns to my Hallan, the tip of her tongue tracing its way up my shaft. This time, when she takes me into her mouth, I cannot hold back. With a roar, I empty myself into her mouth. I am dimly aware I am not supposed to waste my seed in this way, but the pleasure is too much, her touch too clever. She lifts her head to look into my eyes as she swallows, gulping my essence down.

My mate will be my undoing!

21

JAYNE

I think that Rex might like blow jobs.

I was only just able to get the head of his cock into my mouth. He lasted no time at all before he came in great streams down my throat. My poor warrior, he's never had a female pleasure him.

He lies, panting, his iridescent gray skin glinting with sweat. I move back over him, cuddling into his side and gently tracing my finger over his heavily muscled chest. The electric blue markings that encircle his collar bone glow. I'm beginning to understand that they react to his emotions, providing they are positive. He lets out another groan as I run my hand over one, feeling its heat and noting how he shudders at my touch.

For all their genetic engineering, if Rex is anything to go by, Haalux males are sensual beings who love being pleasured. Perhaps that is the point. Perhaps originally, males were supposed to enjoy the mating process before it became tightly controlled. I'm still admiring Rex's heaving chest when his arm snakes around my waist and pulls me to him.

"You're a wicked female, making me spill my seed that way." He murmurs, his orange eyes blazing. "I'm going to have to teach you a lesson."

In a lightning-fast movement, he has me under him and is stripping away the remainder of my clothing, his already hard cock pushing insistently at my entrance. I spread my legs to allow him easy entry. I don't understand what it is that makes me want this alien male, but I do. I want him inside me, close to me and to take me hard and fast. I gasp out in pleasure as he slips into me in one single long stroke, filling me completely.

"Now what are you going to do?" He growls, lust written all over his face as he stares down at me.

I wrap my legs around his slim waist and push my hips up towards him, allowing him to go even deeper. His eyes widen at the feeling, and he groans.

"And how about you, Rex? What are you going to do?" I retort, placing my hand on the side of his face.

He drops his head to devour my mouth with his. His tongue whips, entwining with mine as he grinds against me. I can feel every single inch of him as he withdraws and circles his hips as he moves back inside me. I tilt my pelvis and let my legs drop to give him even better access, and he drives in hard. Each thrust becomes more insistent. Every touch brings me closer, increases my pleasure until I start to buck, the throbbing in my pussy becoming a wave of ecstasy I'm unable to control. I cling to Rex as my orgasm overtakes me, shuddering through me over and over again. I dimly hear him roar with triumph as he spills his seed for a second time, deep within, his cock throbs and pulses as he empties every last drop inside me.

He props himself on his elbows as he pants. We are hot and sweaty, our orgasms slowly subsiding. As he slowly withdraws his semi-hard member, I shudder in pleasure. Rex gathers me in his arms.

"I don't know what this is that you do to me, but I like it." He admits. "I never expected to enjoy sex, but I find that, with you, I do."

"Just enjoy it?" I query.

He bends his head to kiss me. "More than enjoy it. It is the greatest pleasure."

He has no idea how much that means to me. I want to be something more than I was, than I am, in my final hours. If I can pleasure Rex, make him feel good about himself, then that is what I want to do. I run my fingers through his strange feather hair.

"How long do you reckon we're going to be locked in here?" I trace a finger over one of his markings and, as usual, he responds by closing his eyes in pleasure.

"I expect Jaal will let us be alone for a few more hours." He smiles at me, a wicked smile full of promise.

NERVOUS DOES NOT EVEN COVER how I am feeling. Bile rises in my throat as I stand outside the holo-suite with Rex, waiting to be summonsed. The last twenty-four hours have passed by in a flash. I've not even had time to process my feelings from last night.

Rex and I had made love over and over whilst we were supposedly trapped in my room. I could not get enough of his body, and he seemed to be making up for lost time. The urgency in which he took me was reciprocated. As I lay in his arms, his breath soft and even on my neck, I already knew winning this trial has become less about saving my life and more about being with him, not that I even know if that is possible.

I see Dagar striding down the corridor towards us, and Rex tucks me behind him. Dagar does not even look at me. He simply lets out a derisory snort as he whisks into the holo-suite. I close my eyes to remember what the Chamber looked like in order not to appear too much in awe.

"It is time," Rex says, grimly.

He has hardly spoken since he left my room, following the all clear from Jaal that allowed us to emerge. He had said he would need to send a relief subordinate, and a young Haalux warrior had sat in his chair, looking bored, until Rex had come to collect me.

The doors to the holo-suite slide open, and Rex enters, with me following. A wall of noise hits me. Unlike last time, the Chamber is full of Haalux males, all represented in digital form. They talk loudly amongst themselves.

As I enter the noise gets louder. It becomes a roar as they see their accused stumbling, blinking into the imposing chamber. I lift my head higher. My stomach might be churning, my palms slick with sweat, but I'm not afraid. I've prepared my case, and I have Rex. He leads me to the small plinth, and I take my position. He moves away from me but still within sight. I'm on my own, and I push down the fear inside me, like I've done countless times facing various judges in my professional capacity. I always said that the day I wasn't nervous going into a courtroom was the day that I lost a case. With the level of terror I'm feeling, I should storm this trial and the entire of the Haalux Empire should go free.

The sound in the room gradually dies down until it comes to an abrupt halt. All the Assembly looks up, and I follow their gaze.

High above us, three hooded figures move to take their seats. The Council of Three have arrived.

"Dagar?" A metallic sounding voice rings out. "You will begin."

I cannot tell if the voice has come from the Council or elsewhere, but Dagar steps forward, an evil grin on his face as he looks me up and down.

"Honored *Tesei*," He bows low. "I present the accused female," he points at me. "She murdered Ambassador Roi in cold blood. She refuses to confess despite the evidence against her. I move that she is condemned and disposed of."

There is a loud murmur that moves through the assembled ranks of the Haalux. As an opening statement goes, I have to accept that it was to the point, if a little lacking in detail.

He turns to me.

"You accept that you have been taking illegal narcotics and have no memory of your recent whereabouts?" Dagar fires out at me.

"I accept that I have no recent memories due to the drugs I was given, not that I took the drugs willingly."

"You accept that as a result of the influence of the drugs, you could have been made to do anything?" Dagar smiles nastily at me.

"I have no memory, presumably that could happen. I'm just a human, up until recently I wasn't even aware of the Haalux Empire. The technology that you have in your galaxy is beyond me." I attempt to look and sound innocent, although what I am saying isn't really helping.

"You accept that the footage of the assassination clearly shows that you were present?" Dagar says with a flourish, his killer blow.

"No, I do not." My voice cracks, and I squeak instead of sounding confident. I clear my throat try again. "Can you confirm that the footage is all the evidence you have that I am guilty?"

I fix my gaze on Dagar, and to his credit he doesn't flinch; although, that might be because he doesn't understand the importance of the question.

"That is all the evidence we need, female!" He barks at me.

I turn away from him and address the Council of Three, hidden in darkness on their balcony.

"Honored *Tesei*, I request that the evidence against me is shown to the Assembly."

"You *want* it shown?" Dagar hisses across at me, a look of surprise on his face.

"I want it shown so that everyone sees what I am accused of and the evidence against me." I try and stand up straight, to show I am not afraid, even though my legs are shaking.

"Very well."

A screen appears within the chamber, hovering just below where the Council of Three sit. The now familiar footage of the assassination starts to run. It still sickens me to see the ambassador die. From what Dagar has told me, with relish, the poison would have made his death extremely painful. Broadcasting the footage to the assembled council members and the Council of Three was a calculated risk on my part.

"As you can see, Honored *Tesei*, the female was clearly at the scene and fired the dart that killed Ambassador Roi." Dagar says, smugly. "The evidence is overwhelming."

"But is it?" I retort, spinning the stylus that I have been using on my data pad in my right hand, as I always do when I am nervous.

Rex has shown me how to control the footage, although as I look down on my screen, I am struggling to see the controls. I take in a deep breath, trying to get my fear under control.

"As you will see at this point, the murderer raises the dart gun," I scroll through the footage and freeze the screen at the point that the figure in the corner of the screen lifts the gun. "I respectfully submit that this cannot be me."

"What do you mean?" Dagar shouts. He immediately scrolls forward to the point where my face is visible. "That is you! There is no doubt."

"There is a doubt, I'm getting to that part, if you'll be patient." I take control of the screen and scroll back.

There is a slight murmur of laughter around the Assembly as Dagar looks rather taken aback by my dismissal. I fumble at my stylus and it drops to the floor, rolling out of my reach. My opponent snorts at me, taking a cheap shot at my misfortune.

"Commander Rexitor?" I call out softly.

Rex straightens and reaches into the pocket of his tunic. He tosses across a new stylus, which I catch easily in my right hand.

"The doubt that this individual in the footage is me has already been sown, Honored *Tesei*."

"Explain, female!" The voice that booms out is so loud I nearly cover my ears.

"As you can see," I try to take my time, to still my thumping heart. "The murderer holds the dart gun in his left hand." I use the controls to draw a shaky circle on the footage, then I hold up the stylus. "But as has just been demonstrated to you, I am right-handed."

A slow buzz starts within the assembly.

"Medic Jaal will confirm that as a species, humans are predisposed to favoring one hand over the other. We are inferior in that way. This means that there is no way I could have made a shot at that distance with my left hand."

The buzz ramps up becoming a cacophony of questioning voices.

"Honored *Tesei*, the footage has been tampered with. I am innocent and I seek clemency!" I shout out as loudly as I can above the noise.

There is a grinding, ripping noise and the entire room tilts alarmingly. The holo projectors stutter and the chamber flickers before it disappears altogether, leaving just me, Rex and Dagar in a white room. The ship lurches again and I'm unable to stay on my feet. Rex reaches me in a couple of strides and scoops me up.

"We're under attack." He says, calmly. His orange eyes are hard and focussed. "Follow me."

22

REX

I was in awe of my mate in the Chamber. She had explained her defense and once she had pointed out that the footage was, as she put it, 'flipped', meaning that it had been tampered with so that the image was swapped, so that left became right and right left. Once that flaw had been seen, it was immediately clear that the evidence was faked.

An impressive fake, but a fake nonetheless.

It was looking like she may have won over the assembly, right up until something hit the *Excelsior*. The way she moved indicated to me it wasn't a warning shot. The last blast knocked Jayne off her feet, and I'm quick to help her up, ignoring the look that Dagar gives me.

Once we are out in the corridor, the alarms shriek. I grab a subordinate as he rushes past.

"Status!" I demand of the wide-eyed young warrior.

"Sir! He snaps to attention, clearly glad to see a senior member of staff. "We are under attack!"

"I am aware of that, warrior. Who is attacking us?" I ask him, careful to keep my temper under control as best I can. Jayne coughs as smoke starts to fill the corridor, and I want to check on her.

"No one knows, Sir!" He stumbles over his words, worried his answer isn't good enough for me. It is good enough.

"Get to your post." I order, and he rushes away with some relief.

"I need to get to the bridge," Jayne has her hand over her nose and mouth, her eyes streaming. "Can you make it through this? The emergency extraction will begin operating shortly." She nods at me.

I weigh up my options in taking Jayne with me. She has proved her innocence as far as I'm concerned. The trial will have been recorded up until we lost the connection. Having briefly considered returning her to the med bay, I know Jaal will be overrun. Regardless, I need her by my side. I can't imagine not being with her, not now I can fully claim her as mine.

The extraction system whines into action and the smoke starts to clear. I take Jayne's hand and lead her through the ship as quickly as I can. We are rocked by a further explosion, and I'm thrown to the floor. The Excelsior starts to list to one side. I'm quickly on my feet, ready to race down the corridor, when I see Jayne has not managed to get up.

"Rex!" She cries out, lifting one of her hands. It is covered in blood from a large gash on her leg.

"Fuck!" I swear involuntarily as I quickly gather her in my arms. It looks like we are going to the med bay anyway.

As I had predicted, the med bay is rapidly filling with injured warriors. Mostly plasma burns, presumably from being close to the explosion sites.

"I'll be fine, Rex. You go to the bridge. It's where you're needed." Jayne says into my ear.

I reluctantly set her down, and she holds onto the wall behind her. I grab an orderly.

"Find Jaal, my mate needs treatment." I point at Jayne. His eyes flare, but he hurries away into the melee.

Wrapping my arms around Jayne, I press my forehead against hers.

"I don't want to leave you." I breathe, sucking in her delicious scent.

"And I don't want to die in space. I need you to find out what is going on and to stop it." She says, her blue eyes sparking at me.

This is why she is still alive, why she is innocent. This is the mate I always wanted. In that moment, I know I love her.

"Let her go, Commander. She needs treatment." Jaal chuckles behind me. He's remarkably calm given the chaos around him. "She's safe with me." He reassures me.

Reluctantly I release her, but not before I have taken her sweet lips into mine and had a taste of what is to come. She pants delightfully under me as I let her go. Her gaze doesn't leave me as Jaal helps her away. With my mate in safe hands, I stride through the ship, heading to the bridge.

"Commander Rexitor!" The Captain shouts over at me as I enter. "Where have you been?"

"Sir, I was required to get the human to safety."

"You dealt with your prisoner at the expense of your ship?" He asks, incredulously.

"I believe the trial has proven that she is innocent, Sir. She is no longer a prisoner."

The Captain stares at me for a very long time. "That is not the report I received."

"Then your report was incorrect." I return, evenly.

He takes a breath as if about to speak when the ship is rocked by a further blast.

"Who is firing on us?" I yell out across the bridge, "Why are we not returning fire?" I ask the Helm.

"We would if we could see or detect an assailant. There is nothing to fire upon!" He replies.

"Sirs!" One of my warrior subordinates shouts through the smoke that has started to fill the bridge, "We are being boarded by unknown assailants! Airlock twenty-three."

"Security party to me!" I grab a blaster from the armory kept on the bridge and don't even need to look behind me to know my warriors are falling in as we race out of the bridge and towards the airlock which is being breached.

23

JAYNE

I watch Rex stride away, and it takes everything I have not to run after him. If I could have run. I've no idea what I cut myself on, but it's deep, and there's no way my leg can take my weight. When he fixed his gorgeous eyes on me, it was as if he was ensuring my image was burned in his brain. My alien warrior, proud, handsome and strong. I want him by my side forever.

"Let's have a look at you," Jaal's kind voice breaks into my thoughts.

He helps me over to a vacant pod, not that there are many left. Most are filled with Haalux males, their eyes glazed in pain.

"I'll be fine, Jaal, go and help your warriors." I try to push him away.

"My warriors are made of tough stuff, Jayne." He ignores my hands and starts to spray something over my wound. It stops the bleeding immediately and must have a pain killing effect as the throbbing eases. "There, all done."

A further blast rocks the ship, and Jaal glances around him, making sure that no one who is already injured has been hurt further. A new stream of casualties appears.

"I should put you in your pod," He hesitates. "Rex'll never forgive me if anything happens to you."

"I'll be fine, Jaal, just go." I wave him away. He gives me a grateful look and hurries away.

There is a groan from the pod next to me. A very young warrior occupies it. His eyes are almost yellow and his Haalan markings are not as pronounced as Rex. He shakes uncontrollably, his tunic ripped and burnt away, his gray skin blistered horribly.

"Hey there," I say, crouching down beside him. He stares at me, probably wondering if he is hallucinating. "How are you doing?"

"It hurts," his teeth chatter.

"I'll get Jaal to give you something for the pain, sweetheart." I take his hand.

"A warrior does not give in to pain." He grits his teeth but does not move his hand from mine.

"A warrior needs to ensure he gets well enough to fight again," I tell him. His yellow eyes fill with tears, and I wonder just how young he is. "It's going to be okay, honey."

All my life, I wanted to help people, to fight on the side of justice. That all corrupted when my last case imploded. My good work thrown away for one stupid mistake. I'm not going to let it happen again. I am going to be a better person and follow the example set by Rex. I give the young warrior's hand a pat and look around for Jaal. I spot him on the other side of the med bay. Now the pain in my leg has gone, I wind my way through the injured to get to him.

"Jaal?" I call out as I get close. I'm pass by the door to the corridor as I head towards him.

It opens, but rather than admitting more wounded, there are several very large, very imposing green skinned aliens. Big tusks curl out from their protruding lower jaws. They are dressed in loincloths, their naked chests crisscrossed with bandoliers. They all hold menacing looking black blaster weapons. One of them sees me and reaches out, grabbing hold of my arm before I can twist out of his way. He pulls me out into the corridor, clutching me to his chest.

I squirm, struggle, and attempt to bite, but he is not letting go as he half carries, half drags me with him. There is a zipping sound and an explosion. One of the green aliens is thrown to the side, a huge wound appearing on his arm. He barely notices. The three green aliens return fire at the Haalux that have spotted them in the corridor.

"Get Commander Rexitor!" I yell back at them. "Please! Get Rex!"

I'm not sure if they even heard me over the sound of the battle, and I can't tell who is winning, only that I am being dragged away by the three massive aliens. My struggling is having no effect other than to piss off my captor, who punches me in the side of my head, and I see stars. By the time I have recovered my senses, we are in what appears to be a dead end and the battle still rages. There is a hissing sound and I spot a large, heavy door rolling back. We are at an airlock. They are going to take me off the ship.

I'm being abducted again, and Rex is nowhere to be seen.

24

REX

The Grolix had already breached the airlock by the time my team arrived. Disgusting creatures, mercenaries for hire. Their presence soils the *Excelsior* and gives me no indication as to who might be behind this attack. We quickly dispatch them and secure the door.

"*Commander Rexitor,*" My comm signals me urgently, "*there is another breach, airlock sixty-three. Heavy fire, Security team Nine require back up!*"

That's the airlock closest to Jayne in the med bay. My stomach hits my boots. I have to get to her.

"Airlock sixty-three!" I bark, already running as fast as I can in the direction of the breach and my mate.

By the time we reach the med bay, several security teams are trying to pin down the enemy. I direct my team to engage and race to check on Jayne.

"They took her Rex, I'm sorry," Jaal says, holding out his hands, a look of desperation on his face.

Red flashes across my vision. *They took my mate.* There is no way any dirty Grolix is getting their filthy claws on her.

"Be careful, Rex," Jaal calls out behind me. "There's more to this-" His words are lost in a burst of blaster fire.

I stride down the corridor to where the battle is concentrated. My mind is completely clear. I will get to Jayne, no matter what. Blaster shots zip past me, tearing at my uniform. I take a hit in the shoulder, but don't feel any pain. All I know is I will get to her. I take down a couple of Grolix stragglers; they always work in numbers. The ugly beings crash to the floor and are still. It is only after I round the corner into the next corridor that I realize they are retreating to another airlock. They still have Jayne, and they intend on getting away.

In front of me several Grolix bundle a bucking figure through the airlock.

"Rex!" I hear Jayne's voice, loud and clear, ringing towards me.

It urges me on, but as I reach the end of the corridor, the airlock slams shut. I'm unable to slow my pace and I hit it at full speed just as they drag Jayne through the second door and onto their ship. I slam my hand on the airlock release mechanism as the external door closes. The inner door alarm chimes; it won't open whilst the other ship is engaged. I take my blaster and fire at the mechanism over and over until it releases and I'm in the airlock, racing for the second door.

As I reach it, the Grolix ship disengages. I see Jayne through the window. She's still fighting with the big, green bastards. She squirms free and manages to get back to the window of their airlock. I see her shouting my name as she looks back at the *Excelsior*. The Grolix ship winks out of existence as I hammer on the airlock door, every fibre of my being needing to get to my mate.

"Drop your weapon, Rexitor," I hear Dagar's voice behind me and turn to face him.

His blaster is trained on me. Behind him are a number of his warriors, all of whom have their weapons covering my every move. I'm outnumbered. I toss my blaster at his feet.

"What the fuck are you playing at, Dagar? Where is the Captain? We need to get after that ship!" I growl.

"We're doing nothing of the sort, traitor!" Dagar snarls.

He motions at me with his blaster, and I raise my hands, stepping back into the main ship. Captain Clarin is waiting for me.

"I'm disappointed in you Rexitor. I believed in you and gave you a chance to prove yourself as an honourable Haalux warrior. I ignored your obvious shortcomings, and you have repaid me, and the Empire with treachery." He spits out.

"I have done nothing of the sort, Captain, I have the utmost respect for the Empire. You know that! I was following your orders!"

"And yet you collude with the prisoner, a murderer no less, to attack the flagship of the Empire and orchestrate her escape!" The Captain's eyes are blazing with anger. Dagar stands beside him looking smug.

"She's not a murderer. She proved her innocence!" I appeal to him.

"That is not the case, Rexitor. The trial was interrupted. On your orders!" Dagar intervenes with a sneer.

Jaal steps up behind the Captain and whispers something in his ear.

"Medic Jaal advises me that your erratic behavior is due to your Zycle being triggered early by the presence of the female." The Captain pinches the bridge of his nose, the anger gone. "You are therefore relieved of duty and will be placed in Zycle-stasis until we return to Haalux."

I'm not sure what I dislike more, the look of disappointment on the Captain's face, or the look of disdain on Dagar's.

Jaal stares me straight in the eye. The corner of his mouth quirks up. He steps forward and in a swift movement, he has pressed a hypo-syringe onto my bare flesh, where my tunic has been ripped away in the fight. The hiss of the drug delivery is the last thing I hear before the darkness descends.

25

JAYNE

The big green aliens were not messing about. As soon as they had me on their ship, they sedated me. When I awoke in a white, windowless cell, the last thing I remembered was Rex's face, staring at me through the porthole. The look of desolation I saw ripped at my soul. He had said I was his mate and that obviously meant something to him.

And he meant something to me. The first person to believe in me for a long time.

Over the next few days, my only interaction with the horrible green aliens was the food that was shoved into my cell through a hatch. Then, without warning, the cell had filled with a weird pink mist and I had passed out.

I stretch and yawn and find I'm not in a cell anymore. Instead, I'm on a nice bed, in a light and airy room and wearing a light nightdress. The smell of fresh air and vegetation blows in on a breeze coming through an open window, which tells me I'm not in space. The unusual scent, however, is a pretty good indication I'm not back on Earth.

The room itself is rather ordinary. White walls, muslin-like material hangs at the windows, an egg shaped object in one corner that has doors, which I assume is some sort of closet. A glass of water and a plate of what looked like fruit sits on the nightstand next to me. My stomach growls and I slurp greedily at the water. The fruit is refreshing and tastes a lot like apple. I gratefully hoover it down.

Having dealt with my hunger, I face the inevitable. I'm going to have to leave the bed and explore, maybe even face some of those big green buggers. A sob rises in my throat. I'd already resigned myself to not returning to Earth, but being with Rex had given me hope that perhaps my life might have changed for the better. He is gone and I am alone again. I have no option. I'm going to have to fend for myself. I've done it before.

The nagging voice at the back of my brain points out just how well that had worked last time.

Having steeled myself and done my best to ignore my inner bitch, I climb out of the bed and check the egg-shaped closet. It contains a couple of white shift dresses. In the bottom was a small cubby hole that contained underwear. Well, large, white nana knickers. There was nothing that resembled a bra.

"Commando or no?" I say to myself.

As much as I was clearly about to start a new phase in my life, I decide not to go knickerless. Best to face the new day with a good sturdy pair of nana knickers.

Dressed, I open the bedroom door and peer out. It leads directly into another, larger room that is furnished as simply as the bedroom. At one end is a couch and a low table set on a multi colored rug. At the other end is a kitchen area with a small round dining table.

Sat at the table with her back to me is a female alien that makes me do a double take. Her skin is a shocking mauve colour, that is jarringly offset by long blue hair that falls down her back. I see she's reading on a device that looks very much like a tablet. She turns to see me in the doorway and blinks her large dark eyes that take up a huge amount of her head, a head that is perched on a long slim neck.

"Welcome, sweet one," She walks over to me and wraps her thin arms around me in an embrace, "Welcome to Katahrr."

"I can't stay here," I say as she releases me from her angular hug. "I need to get back to my-"

I hesitate, what exactly was Rex to me? He called me his mate on a couple of occasions, but the word is as alien as he is. I'm not sure I could call him a 'boyfriend' as that certainly doesn't fit the bill for the massive warrior that he is. All I know is that he had become my world, and at that moment, it physically hurts me to be away from him.

"I need to get back to the Haalux Empire." I continue, which seems a good a starting point as I can muster. "I have to clear my name."

"No way off Katahrr." The female shrugs. "They collect our stones every turn. Maybe some passengers, maybe some wares. That is all."

My translation chip struggles with her language, her words coming over in short bursts.

"How long is a turn?"

She holds up her hand, extends her four fingers and points outside with her other hand. "Four hundred of light to dark."

I've no idea how long a day lasts, but if it was close to an Earth day, that's a long time before any ship comes.

"When's the next collection?"

"Oh, not for many lights." She smiles at me, or at least the tiny corners of her small mouth twitch up. "You no worry. You safe. The Grolix say keep you safe."

"The Grolix? Big guys, green, bad teeth? Did they bring me here?" She nods her head, apparently not bothered that they would do something like that.

"I am Natiydi," She points to herself. "I help you here."

I'm reeling at the knowledge that I've been deliberately brought to this place and marooned without hope of escape. Natiydi stares at me with her liquid eyes. I realize I'm being rude.

"I'm Jayne," I give her my very best smile, "If I can't travel off this planet, Katah - "

"Katahrr," Natiydi corrects me.

"Katahrr - can I contact someone to come and get me?" I say, hopefully.

"No possible. Our technology..." She shakes her head sadly, spreading her long slim fingers and touching her device. "Not good enough. But you safe here." She brightens. "Let me show you!"

With that, she takes my hand in hers and leads me out of the open door from the dwelling into the fragrant air of her planet.

26

REX

By suggesting to the Captain that I had entered my Zycle, Jaal has bought me some precious time. He knocked me out for long enough to have me placed in the Zycle room with the other males awaiting transport back to Haalux. I awake, strapped into an extractor with a clear head and Forat crouching beside me.

"What *have* you been up to, Commander?" He chuckles under his breath.

"Fuck you, Forat. Get me off this thing." I mutter, struggling to extract myself from the machine.

All around me, sedated males release groans that are part pain and part satisfaction. At least Jaal didn't hook me up to the extractor, which, given his odd sense of humor, he might just have done, and I'm grateful for small mercies. With Forat's help, I untangle myself and slide off the cradle. He hands me some clothing as being naked was the one thing Jaal has not spared me.

"Where is my uniform?" I pulled on the off-duty trousers and top Forat has brought.

"For now, Rex, you're going to have to suffer through not being the big shot Commander. Not if you want to get off this rust bucket and find your mate." Forat hisses at me.

"How do you-?" I cease my question when I see the look Forat gives me.

"It was pretty damn obvious, Rex. And for what it's worth, she's a real beauty and with brains, too. You're a lucky Haalux!" I swell with pride at his words; although, it's immediately punctured by my last memory of Jayne, crying out my name as she was taken from me.

"I have to find her, Forat," I grasp at his clothing, desperation overtaking me. "I have to!"

"You will, Rex, if I have anything to do with it." He grips at my forearm as I stare into his dark orange eyes, serious at last. "We've docked with the *Keeper*. I can get you aboard. They've got a cruiser that was confiscated recently from a group of marauders. You can take it. I've arranged it so no one knows it's missing."

I breathe a sigh of relief. If I'd been transported back to Haalux, any chances of escape would have been slim.

"Do you know where she is?" I ask him urgently.

"For fuck's sake, Rex!" He fires out, "One thing at a time. Your mate is part of a much bigger plan, as are you. Why do you think you've ended up here, like this?"

As usual, Forat is right. Like any mated male, I'm so consumed with my desire to find Jayne that I've overlooked very important aspects of my situation, exactly why I was now accused of being a traitor and what the attack on the *Excelsior* meant.

"Let's go!" Forat winks at me. He's a wily old warrior. I know he's deliberately avoided any form of promotion, and for the first time, I'm wondering why.

He checks the corridor outside of the Zycle room and motions me to follow him.

"Dagar and the others are busy providing their reports to the Assembly. This attack on the *Excelsior* has not gone down well." Forat explains as we race through the ship. "The tech that the Grolix were using was far beyond anything we thought they had."

"I don't believe it's their tech, Forat. They're hired guns. They don't invest in anything. Whatever they have, they were given by their employers." Forat leads me into parts of the ship that I don't even recognize.

"I like it when you think outside your Academy training, Rex. I knew there was a reason we were still friends." Forat grins at me.

"I thought you kept me around for my good looks." I respond.

When I lost my Jayne, I thought my heart had cracked. Yet inside me, I know she's still alive and that is enough to spur me on. Imagining having her in my arms, buried in her silken heat has my inner warrior rising again.

"Haalux to Rex?" Forat breaks into my thoughts and I focus on him, "I thought I was going to have to hose you off for a second there, Zycle stud." Forat cackles.

We've reached the very bowels of *Excelsior* and stand in front of a small hatch. Forat swiftly undoes the bolts and the hatch slides to one side.

"You expect me to get in there?" I fold my arms, my muscles bulging.

"You'll fit, Commander. You're not as big as you think." Forat snorts. He shoves a bag at me and grabs my free arm, strapping on a location device. "This is completely incognito. You can link to any network without fear it can be traced back to you. Do not lose it. You'll meet with my contact. he's at the other end." He finishes strapping it on and steps back from me. "There's a data-pad in the bag that tells you everything you need to know. I'm going to have to get back before I'm missed."

He grasps me in an unexpected embrace. "Good luck, Rex. Now get in the pipe!"

He shoves me back towards the hatch. I am momentarily confused about the softness in his dark eyes until there is a sound somewhere nearby.

"Get going!" He hisses.

I shove my shoulders through the opening. It's wider once I'm inside. As I start my crawl, I hear Forat replacing the hatch behind me. The location device emits a soft ping, and I can see I have some way to go before I reach the *Keeper*. Forat neglected to tell me how long the ships would be docked with each other, so I up my pace, checking the device occasionally to chart my progress, until I eventually reach the end of the tube. I bang on the hatch and, after an uncomfortably long wait, I hear sounds of the bolts being removed and the hatch swings open.

A blaster appears, directly in my face.

"Come out slowly."

"I can't get out any other way." I force myself through the opening and land in a heap on the floor, rolling onto my back to look up at whoever is holding the blaster. A strong light shines in my eyes, and then a hand is extended, helping me to my feet.

"Commander Rexitor? I'm Siggy." The light drops away and a young Haalux warrior, all ungainly angles, stands in front of me. To my relief, he holsters the blaster. "I'm Forat's son." He says by way of further explanation.

"Forat has a son?" I reel back.

"He has four sons," Siggy smiles and I can see the resemblance. "I'm the youngest."

"I didn't know he was a mated male."

"He's not," Siggy's smile widens. "I'll let you into a little secret, Commander, I'm not a full Haalux."

I'm unable to stop staring at him. He is the perfect representation of a Haalux warrior with his single Hallan marking. Him not being a full Haalux is something I'm struggling to comprehend.

"I think I'm going to have to leave Forat to explain it all to you. We don't have time right now. The *Keeper* is going to detach from the *Excelsior* shortly and we need to get you onto *Spirit*."

"*Spirit*?" I query.

"The cruiser, didn't my father mention it?" Siggy hands me a small pot.

"He did, not by name though. What's this?" I take the top off the pot, it's full of a strange goo.

"I need to hide you in plain sight. It'll cover your extra Hallan, just to avoid drawing any unnecessary attention." Siggy explains.

"Makes sense." I slather the goo over the lower half of my face. "How do I look?"

"Boring, just like any other Haalux warrior," Siggy shoots me another grin, "come with me."

I follow Siggy through the *Keeper*, a hulk of a Mega-Class transporter ship. I've only been on one twice before and I'm pleased to have a guide. I've been on asteroids smaller than these behemoths. Once we reach the populated areas, I'm glad of the camouflage. None of the other Haalux hurrying around the ship pay us the slightest attention.

Siggy checks a small handheld screen. "We've got to hurry it up, Commander. The *Keeper* is due to detach, and if you are to leave it unnoticed, that's going to be the best time."

We increase our progress to as fast as we can without breaking into a run until we finally reach the dock.

"There you go, *Spirit* awaits." Siggy says.

The sleek confiscated cruiser in front of us is reminiscent of the Hunter-Class vessel that I'd commanded for a time. It had taken me and my loyal band of warriors on many missions, until the last one, the fateful one that had resulted in the loss of most of my team. Thereafter I was reassigned to the *Excelsior*, having to prove myself again.

"It's coded to your DNA, Commander. I'll be in touch via the comm to coordinate your exit. Good luck." Siggy gives me his father's smile again and darts off back into the maze that is the *Keeper*.

I make my way over to *Spirit*. I can't imagine that is the ship's original name, something this fancy will have been through multiple hands, especially if it ended up in the hands of traders. It opens the main door as I approach and I'm quickly at the controls, firing up the engines.

'We are about to detach from the Excelsior,' Siggy's voice comes through on the comm. *'I can disable the dock forcefield for a short time to allow you to exit, then just act like a piece of space debris until we have gone.'*

That makes perfect sense. As Siggy counts down, I ready for my escape. The forcefield shimmers away and I gun the engines, shooting the ship out of the dock. Once outside, I manually pilot it to appear like it is rolling down the side of the *Keeper*. Tumbling over and over into space to freedom and to find my mate.

27

JAYNE

It's been four months. Four months on this bloody planet and not a word from Rex. At least I think it's four months. The days are longer here and there's not much of a change of season. Katahrr is pleasant enough. It reminds me of Austria, all dramatic jagged mountains and lush pastureland. The colors are all skewed and it messes with my mind for a while. Blue grass and white mountains that are not covered in snow took some getting used to. The Katahrr village that I've been dumped in is welcoming, but distant. I obviously look as weird to them as they seem to me.

As Natiydi had indicated, the main work on the planet is quarrying and dressing the white stone that made up the mountains and virtually everything else on the planet. From what I could tell, it is highly prized by other species as a building material. Despite their natural product's obvious appeal, the Katahrrians are not wealthy. They do well as their land is highly fertile. No one goes hungry, but their technology is like Earth tech. The other species that take their stone give them little in return.

I also got the impression, as time passed, that the Grolix had left strict instructions about me that had put the fear of their gods into the villagers. It initially gave me hope that they might return and I might be able to get back to Rex. However, as time passed and nothing changed, I began to mourn him.

Natiydi remains my constant companion. She arrives on my doorstep each morning to prepare food and clean, something I'm not comfortable with though she seemingly ignores any of my attempts to help or put her off. I guess she had been employed to assist me and nothing I do will stop her.

As my grief slowly cripples me, I give up trying to get rid of her. Natiydi grows increasingly concerned as I shun the meals she makes for me, preferring to stare out at the sky or the stars, looking past their twin moons, hoping beyond hope that Rex will come for me.

"You are with child, sweet one." Natiydi says, placing her hand over my slightly distended stomach.

"Not possible!" I laugh at her. "The last male I slept with wasn't even my species, and I have birth control. I've probably picked up a parasite. I need a doctor."

"You are with child," Natiydi repeats, her dark eyes dancing with mirth. "No doctor, midwife."

She takes me to the other side of the village and introduces me to a wrinkly, old female Katahrrian, who cackles alarmingly when she sees me.

I start to feel like I'm in some sort of fairy tale until she leads me inside her dwelling that, as it turns out, is a medical center.

"I was wondering when you would bring me the human," She says to Natiydi, "I said when she first arrived that she would be with child. There's no other reason why those creatures would leave her with us."

She pats the examination bed, "Hop on, sweet one. Let Metildi take a look at you."

I give Natiydi a long-suffering look, which makes her giggle, and then I climb onto the bed obediently.

"I've already told Nat that I can't be pregnant."

"Why? Have you never had sex with a male?" Metildi says as she rummages in a cupboard with her back to me.

"Yes, I've had sex-"

"Recently?" Metildi interrupts.

"Yes, but-"

"Then you could be pregnant." She turns to me with an odd-looking probe in one hand and a screen in the other. I have a sinking feeling as to what she's going to do with the probe.

"That's what I'm trying to tell you. The male I had sex with wasn't even my species." I fold my arms across my chest and ignored the fact that my breasts are definitely larger than they had been a few weeks ago.

Metildi cackles again. "What makes you think that you are unable to breed with another species?"

"Well, the birth control I am on would make it pretty hard to breed with my own species for a start." I say, smugly.

"I'll be the judge of that, sweet one." Metildi switches on the screen and starts to run the probe over my stomach, stopping here and there as she frowns at the screen.

"You are with child, see-" She turns the screen towards me.

It's there, as clear as day. A tiny jellybean, its little heart beating strongly, a new life grows within me.

"No! It can't be!" I clutch at the screen.

My child. Rex's child. The child he'll never know about unless I can get off this wretched planet.

28

REX

Being a Haalux warrior, even one with my extra Hallan, has its advantages. Most species are swift to give up any information I need. I may be a fearsome warrior in my own right, but as long as the creatures I approach think I have the might of the Empire behind me, it helps them to spill their guts. Fortunately, the trail the Grolix left behind them was easy to follow. My tracking abilities had put me at the top of the Academy; however, they are hardly needed. If you pay a species to do your dirty work, then there will always be loose ends and loose tongues.

I've seen the inside of enough dirty space-taverns to last me a lifetime, but the trail had led to Katahrr, and, I hope, my mate.

Katahrr is supposed to be a peaceful planet, but I'm not taking any chances, not if Jayne is here. So I activate the shielding on my small cruiser and choose an unpopulated area in which to land. I'm going to have a day or so's trek to the nearest village, yet if she is here, it will be more than worth it.

It's taken far too long to track her down. Each day without her has been sheer torture. As warriors we were not taught much about the mating bond. It was expected that, as few of us would experience it, little teaching was necessary. What I have discovered in the long months since I found, and lost, my mate has been both beautiful and painful.

As soon as I step off the ship, something within me snaps into place. Jayne is here. I just *know*.

I sling my pack over my shoulder and check my wrist mounted guidance system. It shows me the nearest settlement. If I keep up a good pace, I should be there by dark. If my luck improves, I may even have my mate in my arms by tomorrow. It's the thought that has me striding out into the dark blue forest ahead of me as quickly as I can.

The terrain is easy going. The blue forest gives way to rolling pastures of blue grass dotted with native farm animals. Six legged ruminant creatures, their shiny black wing casings clipped to make them easier to handle. They regard me steadily with their three dull eyes, chewing on the blue grass as I pass. The settlement I aim for appears at the end of a long valley. My pace had been even better than I'd thought and I will reach it long before nightfall.

I reach the outskirts of the village. The place is relatively quiet and I make my way to the main square looking for the busiest place. A number of the local females, all mauve skin and bright blue hair, are congregated outside of a shop selling foodstuffs. There's a distinct lack of males, who are presumably away in the Katahrrian quarries.

"I am Rexitor of Haalux. I am looking for my mate, a human female. I believe she was left here by the Grolix scum?"

The females blink their big dark eyes in alarm. I might have gone too far with the scum remark.

"Have any of you heard of a human on Katahrr? They have soft pink skin. My mate has long hair the color of the Haalux nebula and eyes like the sky." I try, looking around at the gathered Katahrrians hopefully.

One of the females steps forward. "You sound like a male looking for his mate. Follow me." She quirks her small mouth in what seems to be a smile as she beckons me.

I follow her through the village to a small dwelling on the outskirts. The place seems deserted, and I'm beginning to wonder if the locals are as friendly as they seem. She opens the front door and enters. I check my blaster and follow her.

Standing in the room is my Jayne. She is dressed in a simple white shift, one hand splayed over her rounded belly. Her long hair is much longer, falling in soft waves down her back. She looks absolutely gorgeous, glowing with her pregnancy.

I'm across the room in a single stride, only to be stopped in my tracks by the oddest creature I have ever seen. It streaks past Jayne and halts at my feet. It's small, black and as I look at it, it grows into a large spiky ball whilst emitting a loud hissing spitting sound. I move to one side to get to my mate and it follows me, emitting a wail as I try to get past it.

All I want is to get to my beautiful mate, who watches the whole scene as coolly as she faced down the Council all those months ago. I again try to get past the creature, who seems to be expanding in front of my eyes. As I put out my hand to try and move it, there is a crackle and a spark which hits me with a jolt, and I pull my hand away immediately.

"Fitz, leave!" Jayne calls out.

The thing transforms into a long streak of black that partly flows, partly scampers over to her, swirling its way over her body until it takes up residence around her neck. It vibrates as she strokes it, and it is only now I can see its deep red eyes. Its blunt head snuffles at her and then licks at her hand, exposing two rows of needle-sharp teeth.

"Rex," She eyes me with a guarded gaze, her voice only just audible. "I thought you'd never come."

29

JAYNE

"I thought you'd never come." I whisper.

When I see Rex standing in the doorway, his bulk filling the frame, I think I might be dreaming. As soon as she realizes that I know Rex, Nat bowed her head and left us, but I had forgotten about Fitz. He doesn't take kindly to strangers and Rex is most definitely strange to him.

"What on Haalux is that?" He steps towards me, peering at Fitz, intrigued.

"The Katahrrians call them Masca. They are considered rare as they were once hunted for their fur. I found this one as an injured kit. I cared for him until he was strong enough to go back to the wild." I give Fitz a stroke and he hums gently. "But he decided to stick around, and I decided to let him." I stare hard at Rex, hoping he gets the message.

"*Kedves*, my mate," Rex pleads, "I'm sorry." He steps closer and Fitz hisses in alarm.

I quiet him and gently lift him from around my neck, placing him on the bed where he immediately curls into a sleek ball. I take a few steps towards Rex.

"Where were you?" I thump my hands on his heavily muscled chest.

He wants to be in my arms but instead takes a step back at my reaction. I get my first proper look at him. He's bigger, if that's even possible. Gone is his stiff uniform. Instead, he wears a pair of tight-fitting trousers that leaves little to the imagination as they cling to his muscular thighs. His chest is bare, and he wears a soft biker style jacket that looks like it is made from black suede. Two black leather-like weapons belts crisscross his chest. His hair is shorter, the center feathers raised like a crest. His markings glow as I take him in.

He is as magnificent as I am a rotund ball of pregnancy hormones.

I thought I'd known how much I missed him. Away from the intensity of the trial, I'd wondered what I'd felt for him. Occasionally I wasn't sure if I'd felt anything for him at all and had just imagined our connection. Once I found out I was pregnant, my confusion around what he was to me grew further. I've thought every day what it would be like when Rex came for me, and now he is here. I don't know what to feel.

"I had to find you, *Kedves*. It took time, too much time. Can you ever forgive me?" He holds his hands out to me, his face a picture of misery.

I shake my head and move back from him, one hand on my pregnancy. All I wanted when Rex wasn't here was him. Now he is here. Every emotion my body can muster fights for attention. Anger, desire and fear flood me in bucketloads. I can't pick one out. My vision begins to waver, and I sit down hard on my bed.

Immediately, Rex is next to me. He doesn't try to touch me, but his size and warmth is reassuring.

"Are you okay, my mate?" He asks, his voice rumbling through my chest.

"I get a bit light-headed since this one made her presence known. The midwife says it's normal." I rub my hand over my belly.

"She?" Rex's big, gray hand covers mine.

"We're having a girl, Rex." I look at him and into his stunning orange eyes. I only found out two days ago.

"Then I am complete." He leans into me and captures my lips with his.

This time I don't pull away. I enjoy the feel of his heated skin on mine for the first time in a long time. It's something that has haunted my dreams, waking only to find myself alone. Rex's hand is pushing insistently at my shift and up my thighs towards my heat, his kisses deepening as he wraps his arms around me tighter, his tongue exploring in the same way his hand is drifting closer to my pussy. I can feel his hard shaft pressing against me. My arousal heightens, and I want him.

But I want answers more.

"No!" It takes a huge mental effort to push him away.

He sits back, his eyes half lidded with lust. His trousers leaving absolutely nothing to the imagination. I check myself severely when I spot the bulge.

"What's been going on, Rex? Why was I taken and how come I ended up here?"

30

REX

My desire to reclaim my mate overtook me. After all this time, the thought of burying my cock inside her was overwhelming. I should have known that my intelligent Jayne would want more than mere physicality and I have a lot of explaining to do. It doesn't help that her pet is staring at me with his red eyes, hissing slightly. That certainly takes the edge off.

"I'm sorry, *kevdes*. You deserve answers and you did not deserve to be treated this way." I shift uncomfortably on the bed. Although my lust has diminished, my throbbing cock has not.

"I get the apologies, Rex. I just want to understand a bit more about what's going on." Her head droops, and tears form wet circles on her white shift.

"My sweet mate," I encircle her in my arms, and she melds into me. "Much has happened since you were taken from me."

"I know!" Jayne lets out a soggy laugh and pats her stomach.

"After you were kidnapped—" I suppress the rage boiling within me at the thought of her ever being out of my sight again. "I was accused of being a traitor to the Haalux Empire."

"What the-!" Jayne exclaims, her eyes a stunning blue, wide with shock.

"Well, at least one creature can't imagine that possibility," I smile down at her and tighten my grip on her lush body. "I was fortunate to have both Jaal and my good warrior, Forat, on my side. They assisted me in getting off the *Excelsior*. Then all I had to do was track you down."

"You took your time." Jayne says. I notice that she buries herself just a bit closer to me. I lift her onto my lap and shuffle back so that we are both comfortable on the bed.

"It was you who led me here."

"How did I do that? Did you have some sort of weird stalky tracker on me?" She giggles as I bury my head in her hair to inhale her aroma.

"You said you thought it was odd that a virtually unknown species, one considered to be primitive, would be accused of such a high crime against the Empire. And you were right."

"I'm always right, Rex," Jayne laughs. She seems to be warming up to me and that has to be positive. "So, I was set up?"

"We both were. The attack on the *Excelsior* was a set up too. It was aimed at getting you off the ship before the trial could be completed and to discredit me. Although I'm still not entirely sure why I posed a threat."

Jayne remains quiet as I explain what I have found out in my months trawling the less salubrious stations, asteroids, and planetoids of the galaxy. Initially, because the Grolix ship had used a new and sophisticated cloaking device, the trail to find her had gone cold. With the information that Forat had given me, I was able to track down some unemployed Grolix warriors, who, for a price, were prepared to give me some details about the mission their brethren had undertaken. Jayne, as a rare species, was either remembered or not. Her rarity helped me track her down.

"The warriors I spoke to referred to a species that they called 'The Unseen', as being the instigators of the attack. They seemed to have vast wealth and technology behind them, but apparently not the numbers or the stomach for what needed to be done."

"I still don't understand how a little human like me ends up involved in all this?" Jayne absently stroked the odd creature that had made its way onto her lap, crooning at her touch. I envied it intensely. I place my hand over her expanded stomach protectively.

"Ambassador Roi was not the paragon of a Haalux he was held out to be."

I had found this information out from a rogue trader by the name of Xil. A Ulongi, his species were known as traders, but Xil had turned more in the direction of piracy. I had agreed to help him with a shipment in return for information and a few credits. If I had any hope of returning to the Haalux fleet, it died the moment I ran the illicit goods past one of our Hunter-Class ships onto a nearby planet.

"He was involved in a number of illegal activities, including weapons trading. I believe he was killed to keep him quiet. From all accounts he had become greedy. Those species willing to talk to me about The Unseen indicated that they are cold and ruthless in the extreme. Taking him out solved a problem for them and created one within the Haalux Empire as he was considered a key figure in our talks with our most recently acquired planet, Alinor. Without him the talks were doomed to fail, and we are back to square one."

"I thought the Haalux took the planets they wanted like that anyway, negotiation wasn't your preferred method." Jayne says, gently stroking the back of my hand that is curled over her delicious bump. "The Katarrhian's told me."

"We used to, but there have been moves towards negotiations in recent turns. It was felt that we gained better cooperation from the indigenous species and as such, better access to their resources. It's still not a perfect model. Many planets give in readily because of our reputation, but it's better than it was with decidedly less bloodshed." I explain. "Whoever chose to implicate you in his killing wanted to cause as much confusion as possible. The introduction of a virtually unknown species meant that no one could really know who was behind the killing. And, as you didn't either, it would cause fractures within the Assembly."

"So, when I was able to prove it wasn't me, everything started to fall apart?" Jayne asks, her voice low as she considers what I have been saying.

"It was no coincidence we were attacked at that point."

"So what happens now?" She shifts herself on me, and her scent is almost overwhelming.

I look down into her eyes and see that her mind is eased for the time being. We spent so little time together, yet I already know her.

'Whatever you want, my delicious mate." I gaze at her, beautiful, sensual, and plump.

I have accepted that she is my mate and we are bonded, but I don't know if she has, or that humans even have such a thing. However, right now, I only know that I have to claim her lush body, ripe with my child. As if she has read my mind, she sits forward and pulls her dress over her head, kneeling to face me.

Her gorgeous breasts bob just above her neat pregnancy. Her nipples have darkened to a deep red color, ready for my tongue. She plucks at my weapons belts, and I remove them, along with my jacket, then I reach for her. My fingers caress her soft, creamy flesh, cupping her breasts and sweeping my thumbs over her distended peaks. She lets out a low moan at my touch, her eyes closed, and her head thrown back, wanton and needy. I move down her body so I can properly capture her new form. Her protruding belly is warm and yielding. She is full of my child and the mere thought causes my already hard cock to stiffen further.

31

JAYNE

I wanted answers, and I got some. All the time Rex spoke I struggled to concentrate.

He's called me his mate on a couple of occasions, but I'm not sure I know what that means. He came for me, and he didn't baulk when he saw I was pregnant, so that has to be a good thing. Not that I would know a good thing given I've actively avoided relationships, preferring to concentrate on my career. Up until now, that had appeared to be a waste of ovaries.

I'm still not entirely sure how I got pregnant. What with the coil and the fact that Rex and I are completely different species, it seems highly unlikely. However, Metildi has told me that there is no sign of my birth control and I'm beginning to wonder if Jaal had a hand in my expanding stomach.

I've spent my entire life living for the future, for my career and for others, but I'm still not sure if what I want now is to spend the rest of it in the arms of an alien, bringing up his children, however good it feels. And yet, wrapped in his arms with the scent of him, leathery and musky, listening to his voice, deep and gruff, it feels like home. Maybe I should let go of my stupid control and roll with it.

Rex stares down at me, and I can't hold off any longer. If I don't get some of that gorgeous alien muscle, I think I might explode. It's been too long, and my nights have been lonely, even with Fitz to keep me company.

I whip off my dress and turn to face him, pulling away his weapons slings and jacket. His eyes fill with lust as he takes in my new pregnant form. His hands move to caress me, drifting over my oh-so-sensitive nipples with a featherlight touch that pulls a moan of pleasure from my lips. As he runs over my burgeoning pregnancy, I've never felt so big or so sexy. Judging by what strains in his pants, Rex can't get enough of me, regardless of my new shape.

"My beautiful mate." He murmurs with awe as he explores my body, leaning in to capture my lips with a kiss that leaves me panting.

He kisses his way down my neck until he reaches my breasts, nuzzling at my nipple, he sweeps his tongue across it tentatively. I whimper in response, arching my back, pushing myself at him, grasping at his head, my fingers entwining in his soft feathers. He looks up at me through his lashes as he tongues at me, orange eyes full of wickedness and promise as to what he is going to do to me. He slips a hand between my thighs and my knickers are gone in a flash. He starts to explore my soaking folds. His fingers finding my needy clit, he circles the hard nub, teasing me as he continues to work on my breasts. I fumble at his trousers, wanting to get my hands around his big cock.

The beast is swiftly released, and Rex lets out a groan of pleasure as I work my hands over his shaft. The Hallan markings hot against my skin as his arousal mounts further. He redoubles his efforts on my clit, sliding in thick digit inside me, while his thumb continues a gentle pressure and movement that threatens to bring me to orgasm before I can ride his delicious cock.

"I want you, Rex. I need you," I whisper, cupping his heavy balls, squeezing and massaging them as his hips buck at me.

Rex wraps himself around me, his fingers sliding deeper into my pussy, pumping at me. He lifts me by my waist, and I straddle him, my arms around his neck as his massive member pushes at my soft folds. Our eyes lock as I push down, and he breaches my entrance.

My pussy envelopes him in a wet, tight embrace, and he lets out a low growl once I work my way to the base of his cock, feeling every ridge as I go down over him. He fills me entirely; his eyes burn as he begins to grind his hips against mine.

"Wicked mate!" He thrusts into me, unable to hold back any longer, wrapping his arms around my expanded form and clutching me to him.

He is wild and unrelenting, his hungry cock plundering my soft, wet channel. He had only just discovered that his sexual side was desirable when we were ripped apart, and his desire to reclaim me is evident in every movement. Rex throws me on my back and rises over me, slowing his strokes as he stares down at me. His eyes heat as he takes in my changed form. He watches himself slipping in and out, marveling at our connection, and then he drops his head, his mouth plundering mine. Our tongues entwine and he pushes himself deep inside me. I can feel his entire length, his sparking flesh hits my G-spot, and I'm tipped over the edge, my climax suddenly overtaking me.

My entire body convulses against him, and I cry out in ecstasy at the feel of him, his closeness, and the heat of his hard, muscular body against mine. My pussy clamps down hard over him, and Rex groans. His thrusts become irregular, and I feel his hot seed jetting with his orgasm, as I flutter uncontrollably over his thick member. Our breath come in gasps as we pant in unison.

Rex collapses to one side, still buried in me, pressing kisses in my hair, on my ear and down my neck, murmuring something I can't quite hear. I'm just happy to be in his arms once again, feeling the afterglow of an amazing orgasm that he has given me.

Perhaps I'm over thinking things. Maybe I should, for once, roll with it instead of trying to control it.

32

REX

I want to tell my little mate how much it meant to me to claim her properly, now I know about the bond. But her gorgeous orgasm that caused my balls to explode has virtually taken my power of speech. I'm complete as I gather her to me. A mate and a child. I had no idea what it could possibly mean to be a mated male until this moment, and I'd never thought I would. Hallux warriors born of the forced impregnation scheme are not considered mating material.

Jayne snuggles up to me, her sweet female scent surrounding me, and my cock is already hard again for her.

"Looks like I picked an insatiable male," She giggles, squirming against me, shifting her position to let me go deeper.

"And I've got a very fertile mate," I kiss her deeply as I caress her bump.

Jayne pulls back from me, her blue eyes studying my face.

"Does this mean you are mated now?" She asks earnestly, although she rolls her hips against mine and gently bites her lip in the most delightful way.

"I am mated to you, my beautiful *kedves*," I tuck her beneath me and allow my hands to go exploring, wanting to feel myself inside her. "It is fated and cannot be undone." I seek out her heat and press on the hard pearl that brings her so much pleasure.

Jayne lets out a soft sigh.

"Do humans have fated mates?" I ask, pushing myself deeper.

"I don't know about fated mates, but we have something called 'the one'." She pants out as I rub just a touch harder.

"Am I your 'the one', little mate? What can I do to be your 'the one'?" I ask as Jayne lets out a low moan of passion, and I feel her flood over my throbbing cock, her eyelids flickering as she is consumed by her climax. Her back arches and lifting her gorgeous breasts towards my mouth.

I capture a nipple and suck hard on it, knowing they will soon feed my child. The mere thought causes me to hit my own orgasm, hard and fast. I empty myself into her all over again. If this is what it's like being a mated male, then I believe I'm going to be very happy. Jayne snuggles herself against me, her eyes closed and her face a picture of satisfaction. She did not answer my question, but there's time for that later.

We wake each other throughout the night, wanting more intimacy, to be reminded that we have found each other. When I wake in the morning and see her curled up next to me, naked and glowing, I'm still struggling to believe she is real. There had been dark times in the last few months where I'd wondered if I would ever see her beautiful face again.

So much for being the battle-hardened warrior. Looks like being mated sends you gooey.

Jayne's blue eyes open and look up at me. She smiles, stretches out, her belly and breasts arcing as she lifts her arms over her head and yawns. She spots my lustful gaze.

"As much as I want to stay in bed with you, this little one needs feeding. And when I say that, I mean, I need feeding." She grins at me, rubbing at her naked stomach.

"Then I will feed you," I run my hand over her breast and press a long kiss to her lips that leaves her breathless before I jump out of bed to a moan of disappointment. Naughty mate.

I pull on my trousers and make my way into the living area of her tiny dwelling. At the moment, I'm not entirely sure why she was brought here, but at least she is being well cared for. The place is modest and clean. She has been clothed and is obviously being fed and getting medical care for her child. I head towards the meal preparation area and a solid black streak shoots in front of me.

The creature Jayne called Fitz starts its strange crackling ball effect, and it's preventing me from going any further.

"Get out of the way. I need to get food for your mistress," I tell it.

Two red eyes appear in the center of the spiky ball and it makes a low hissing sound. I put out my hand to move it to one side and a jolt of electricity jumps at me with a snap. I instantly recoil, as does the creature. Stalemate.

There is a soft laugh behind me, and I turn to see Jayne stood in the doorway of the bedroom, barefoot. She wears a long white gown open to the waist. It covers her breasts, but her belly is visible as it protrudes over her underwear. I hope the image is burned into my brain. She is so beautiful.

"Immovable object meet unstoppable force." She laughs.

Fitz becomes a long black streak again, shooting across the room, whizzing up her body until it rests on her shoulders again.

"I'm not sure I like your new pet, *kedves*," I start to open various cabinets to find food for my mate.

"If you do a decent breakfast for us both, I know Fitz will be as devoted to you as he is me." Jayne says, taking a seat at the little table. "I'm expecting good things, great warrior." A mischievous smile on her face.

I set to work in the kitchen, which is well equipped. Most of the Katharrian ingredients are recognizable and I'm able to make us a couple of simple dishes.

"Okay, Rex. I admit it, that was impressive." Jayne sits back in her chair, pushing away her empty plate. "Where did you learn to cook like that?"

"Before I was assigned to the *Excelsior*, I captained a Hunter-Class ship with a specialist team. The food dispensers were poorly equipped. None of them could cook and warriors needed feeding to be on their best form. I learned to prepare a few simple dishes things to avoid us all either starving or being poisoned."

Fitz looks up at me from his bowl on the floor, champing his sharp teeth noisily. I had no idea what Masca ate, so I dumped some of the breakfast omelet that I had made for us into a bowl. It looked like it had gone down well, even if the creature was a messy eater. He extends a long blue tongue, licking away the mess from his face, then he swirls up onto my lap, placing his paws on my chest. He starts to swipe his squat head against me. I raise a hand and lower it to touch his fur, tentatively, remembering what happened last time. He is incredibly soft and smooth to the touch, vibrating with energy of some sort. Humming happily, he curls up in my lap.

"Told you!" Jayne laughed. "One meal and Fitz is anyone's!"

33

JAYNE

There's clearly more to Rex than meets the eye. Although what I'm looking at is pretty hot. He's still shirtless, his muscles bunching and shifting under his iridescent skin. His Hallan glow when he realizes I'm checking him out. I think it must be the Haalux version of a blush. I want to know more about him and not because we're about to start a family together, but because the more he reveals about himself, the more I like him.

We're both brand new to relationships. I've only managed a handful of short flings before my career got in the way. Rex seems pretty set on this idea I'm his fated mate, and I can't deny that his belief both excites and frightens me. What happens if he decides he was wrong? I rub at my rounded stomach, full of food and baby. I guess I'm going to have to make good on my promise to myself and roll with it for the time being.

"So-" I watch Rex try to pet Fitz and try to decide whether or not to warn him about touching his head. "Do we stay here as fugitives from the Haalux Empire or what?"

"We can't stay here. You were put here for a reason, and I'm not prepared to risk your safety by hanging around to find out. My ship is around a day's walk from here," Rex eyes my expanding form, "if you think you can make it."

I'm not sure if I'm more relieved to hear that Rex has a way off this god-forsaken planet or irritated that he thinks I'm not up for a short walk.

"I'm pregnant, Rex, not sick. Of course, I can make it!" I snap, just as Rex reaches the wrong spot on Fitz's neck. The Masca poofs up into a black ball of hell, crackles and spits as Rex lets out a yell.

Fitz immediately disappears.

"What the-?" Rex exclaims. "Where did it go?"

"I'm not entirely sure," I admit. "He does that when he's frightened, or occasionally when he's really happy." I shrug my shoulders.

It's all alien to me. I've learned not to take anything at face value anymore. Fitz has kept me sane on more occasions than I like to admit with his funny antics. True to form, I see Fitz's square head peering around the bedroom door and I pat my lap to encourage him back. Rex is silent as he watches the creature streak across the room and settle on me. Fitz croons as I give him scratch behind what passes for his ears.

"We should get going if we're to reach my ship today." Rex says and starts to pull out food items from my kitchen. "Pack what you need, and we'll make a start."

"What about Nat and the others? I don't want to go without saying goodbye?"

"I'm not sure if that's a good idea." Rex stops what he's doing and turns to face me. "I suspect they're in league with the Grolix."

"They're not in league with anyone!" I almost shout, seeing red. "I've taken care of myself up to now. I don't need you dictating my every move!"

He takes a few steps over to me and gently holds my shoulders. "Keeping you safe is my number one priority. It has to be. Even if the Katahrrians mean well, if they say anything, it puts you at risk."

His orange eyes are gentle and kind, even with my stupid, hormonal related outburst. He's right, of course.

"It's just they've been so kind to me," I pout.

"And they have cared for you both well." Rex places a hand over my rounded stomach, a smile playing over his lips. "But we can't trust anyone, not yet, not until we get more information on who took you and why."

"Okay, Rex," I press a kiss to his lips. He looks so handsome and earnest. "I'll get my things."

In the bedroom I wrap up a couple of items of clothing in a sheet and twist it up to make a handle that I can sling over my shoulder. I've only got a single pair of soft leather-like shoes, which I hope will be up for an all day hike. Back in the kitchen, Rex waits for me. Or he's having a staring contest with Fitz. It's difficult to decide which.

"I'm ready, let's go." I cluck my tongue at Fitz, and he swarms up around my shoulders.

"It's coming with us?" Rex asks, mouth open.

Fitz crackles slightly at his tone, electricity buzzing in my ear.

"How do you propose I stop him?" I fix Rex with a stare, petting Fitz, who hums happily.

Amusingly, my clever, resourceful warrior alien looks at a loss. Exactly how do you stop a creature that can disappear at will from following you? I try not to laugh as various emotions flit over Rex's features until his mouth sets in a hard line.

"It can come." He decides.

I am unable to stop myself from laughing out loud. "Come on then, Fitz. Daddy says you can tag along." I waltz out of the door ahead of Rex, swinging my hips and chuckling to myself as he hurries to catch up.

I stop my laughing when he grasps my elbow and steers me in the opposite direction.

34

REX

The Masca is coming with us. I'm sure I saw a look of satisfaction on its face as Jayne walks past me, shaking her hips saucily. She's right, there is virtually nothing I could have done to stop it following us anyway.

At least I got my own back when I saw her heading in the wrong direction.

We are fortunate that her dwelling is on the outskirts of the village. I had virtually walked past it when I arrived yesterday. This means we do not attract any attention as we leave. Jayne keeps up with my pace easily, although I'm walking slower than I usually would. Out in the open, I'm reminded of how small she is compared to me. In the rarified atmosphere of the *Excelsior* our size difference didn't seem so marked. Yet she is dainty and delicate. I sneak a look at her and her face is a picture of determination. Fitz has uncurled himself from his resting place around her neck and is flowing alongside us, his progress a mixture of streaking ahead and long bounding strides. I must admit it's amusing to watch, and I can see why Jayne kept the creature around.

We make good progress. I stop every once in a while to make sure Jayne takes a rest, eats, and drinks. I'm certain that if I didn't do this my stubborn mate would not say a word. It's this quality that has kept her alive so far, and I admire her for it. My wrist mounted direction finder advises me we are not far from my ship. It's just starting to get dark, and we should, just about, reach it before night falls.

"Not far now, *kedves*," I wrap my arm around her shoulders and I find she's shaking.

So much for keeping an eye on her. I toss her into my arms, despite her weak protests. She immediately curls against me.

"Why do you do that to yourself?" I ask, quietly.

"Do what?"

"Push yourself too far. You've nothing to prove to me." I stride on with her nestled comfortably. She weighs almost nothing. I probably could have carried her all the way if she would have let me. Something tells me that would not have been an argument worth having.

"What does *kedves* mean?" She replies with her question, dodging mine. "It doesn't translate."

"It's from ancient Haalux, which is probably why your chip doesn't pick the meaning up. Roughly it means 'fated flower'. Previous generations considered females as precious as the blooms that flowered and were gone fleetingly. They were treated accordingly, with respect and veneration." I explain to her as she traces a finger across one of my Hallan.

"I thought they were treated like that now? You know with the whole Zycle thing?" She says, perceptively.

"Females are treated with respect. But perhaps not with the veneration they once were." As I have found out more about the mating bond, it has shed Haalux mating practices in a new light for me. Jayne presses her lips on my chest and the touch goes straight to my cock. I let out a growl. "If you keep doing that, I'll have to take you right here and right now, naughty mate!"

Jayne giggles and it does nothing to staunch my arousal. We are approaching the clearing in the forest where I left my ship, and I try to get my cock under control. We'll have all the time we need once we are away from Katahrr. Fitz races on ahead of us, a slip of blackness in the undergrowth, until I hear him hiss loudly and the electricity that he crackles with flashes in the gathering gloom. I come to a sudden halt and gently place Jayne on her feet.

"Wait here," I tell her in a low voice. She's already spotted Fitz and nods, her eyes wide with fear.

I pull out my blaster and long thin psi-damascus dagger that is my weapon of choice for close quarter fighting and creep forward, trying to make as little sound as possible. Fitz seems to recognize my hunting stance as he ceases his noise and returns to his normal sleek state, falling into step beside me. As we breach the tree line, I see another ship on the ground next to mine, which is no longer cloaked, a large star shaped blaster mark along one flank. There is no smoke, so I'm hoping there's no permanent damage.

Dotted around the ships are big, green warriors. It looks like the Grolix have returned for Jayne. Finding my ship must have been a bonus for them. Beside me, Fitz lets out a series of low chitters and growls as he stares at the warriors. I agree with him, it's not looking good. Behind me I hear a long shrill scream that chills me to the core.

Jayne!

I race back to where I left her, only to find her struggling in the arms of a particularly ugly Grolix, his tusks broken and yellowing.

"Drop your weapons, Haalux!" The second Grolix orders, "and we won't harm your pretty mate."

Jayne snorts in disgust, and the Grolix holding her squeezes tighter. She lets out a cry of pain. I drop the blaster and the dagger at their feet. The second Grolix picks up the weapons and looks at the dagger enviously.

"Nice," He nods, then motions his own blaster at me, "get going. Hardag is going to love you two."

I walk ahead of the them and we pass out into the clearing, heading towards their ship. The Grolix warriors square up to me as I'm prodded forward when I try to check on Jayne behind me. She looks very pale as she is dragged along. Soon I'm hemmed in on all sides by stinking green flesh. Grolix are always more secure in numbers.

"Where's Hardag?" One of my captors grunts. "I've got prisoners for him, just what he was looking for."

"Hardag is here!" A rough voice rings out across the clearing.

The remainder of the Grolix step aside to reveal probably the biggest warrior I have ever seen. His green flesh marred by multiple scars, some of which appear to have been self-inflicted as they form primitive patterns up his arms. His tusks are filed to sharp points. In common with the rest of his species, he is dressed only in a loincloth. I hear Jayne's intake of breath behind me as Hardag strides towards us.

"Well, well, the Haalux freak and his little mate. Good of you to come to us rather than forcing us to come and find you." Hardag laughs. "Looks like you did the business with her, Commander. Shame, I fancied a bit of human flesh for myself. I hear they have cunts to die for."

He eyes Jayne with a heat that has me launching myself at him. Several Grolix grab me, applying their fists to my torso and head to subdue me. I'm not stopping, not until I can kill Hardag for even looking at my mate. Or until I hear the click of the control collar around my neck. The jolt it gives me has me on my knees.

"Touch her and you'll have me to contend with!" I growl at him.

He plucks Jayne from the ugly Grolix. She twists in his grasp, but he jerks her wrist. She squeaks in pain.

"Mmm," He hums as he runs his massive, clawed hand over her rounded stomach. "All ripe with Haalux young. They will be pleased."

I'm aware they are trying to shock me as I lurch towards Hardag. Anything to get my mate out of his disgusting hands. The look of horror on her face at his touch made me see red. I am going to kill him if it's the last thing I do.

35

JAYNE

My brave warrior crashes to the ground and doesn't move. He was trying to get to me after Hardag started putting his filthy hands on my stomach. I struggle against Hardag, and he lets me go.

"Rex?" I cradle his head in my hands. He's covered in blood from the beating they gave him earlier, and he's out cold. I managed to brush my lips over his before I'm jerked backwards by a big hand.

"I really hit the jackpot!" Hardag grins at me, exposing his jagged yellowing teeth. "And I didn't even have to come and get you." He runs his hands over my body, cupping my breasts and holding my belly. Then without warning, he shoves a thick finger between my thighs and hums with pleasure. "So it is true about human females. Always hot for cock." He grabs his crotch suggestively as I pull away.

"Don't you dare touch me!" I hiss.

"Or what? Your warrior isn't going to be much help to you now." He flicks a hand at Rex and four Grolix hoist him bodily off the ground, carrying him off towards one of the ships. "Anyway, you're destined for a higher purpose, and as such, unfortunately off limits to me and my crew." There is a hunger in his eyes that I don't like. "As long as you behave yourself, that is. Take her to the quarters prepared for her and send in the medic. I need to certify to our paymasters that she is with child."

I'm grabbed by one of the Grolix, and he drags me off towards the same ship as Rex, shoving me up the entry ramp and into the fetid interior. It's a smell I remember from the last time I was taken. Clearly Grolix have no interest in personal hygiene. I see Rex's prone form being taken in one direction as I'm pulled in another. I stumble forward and try not to cry, dipping my head so that the Grolix dragging me can't see. Down at my feet I fleetingly see a familiar lithe black form that winks out of existence soon as I spot him.

"In here, female, enjoy!" My Grolix captor snarls as he opens a door and shoves me inside.

"Fuck you!" I give him the finger as the doors slide shut and his eyes widen at my words.

Well, it's not like I've haven't been in this position before, is it? My life has come full circle back to being a prisoner. I don't see why I should make it easy for the fuckers. A soft chitter behind me means that Fitz has made it into the cell with me. He swirls around me, tucking himself under my ears and making a sound that is like a purring cat as I take in my surroundings. My cell is more like a cabin. There is a bed in the center with bedding along with a small couch. There is even a food dispenser. I've clearly been elevated in the prisoner stakes, or something unpleasant is planned for me. Given the way Hardag looked at me, I'm suspecting the latter. I scratch Fitz behind his ears and sit down on the bed.

I wake to the sound of voices. Not only is my early pregnancy making me tired, the long hike from the Katahrrian village had exhausted me more than I wanted to let on to Rex. Despite my concerns at what was going to happen next, as soon as I hit the bed I was asleep.

A single ugly Grolix stares at me. Stood alongside him is a species I don't recognize. Tall, scarlet skinned with black eyes, he has skin texture that Freddy Kruger would be proud of.

"Are you going to comply, female, or do I need to get him to hold you?" The alien jerks a metal tube he is holding at the Grolix, who grins nastily in a way that I take to mean he would like me not to comply.

"What are you going to do?" I hold my hands up to placate them as the Grolix makes a move towards me, "I'm not saying I won't comply. I just want to know."

"I'm here to check on your young," the red skinned alien says, his severe expression softens slightly. "It's for your own good."

"I doubt that very much, bollock features, but what do you want me to do?" He recoils as my insult slowly translates for me and his expression hardens. I guess he never considered that there are ways of complying that can still make things hard for a captor.

"Lie back and open your legs, female." He orders.

"No," I reply, folding my arms. The big Grolix takes another step towards me. "Not with him here. I'll let you do what you need to, but I'm not spreading my legs in front of that green bastard!" I wave my hand dismissively at the Grolix and refold my arms.

Freddy looks at me and over at the Grolix. I can almost see the gears whirring. He's trying to decide if this will be easier if I'm being held down or not.

"You are dismissed." He finally says.

The Grolix huffs and leaves the cabin as I shuffle back on the bed and remove my knickers. Freddy approaches me, fiddling with something on the metal wand that he is holding. I notice that it's shaped to a blunt point at one end. I've got a good guess at where it's going to go, and I shudder at the indignity. He sits on the bed next to me and parts my legs, bending them at my knees so he can get access.

"This will not be painful, female, but please lie still."

He presses the metal wand at my entrance, twisting it around. He is just about to shove it deeper when Fitz materialises at my shoulder as a spitting black ball of spikes. Freddy recoils just as Fitz sinks his impressive teeth into his arm. I grab the wand and lash out as hard as I can, hitting Freddy with a loud crack over his head. To my complete surprise he keels over on top of me, Fitz still ragging at his arm. I manage to heave him away and he rolls on his back, greeny black blood oozing from a wound where I hit him. It makes me feel slightly nauseous.

"Fitz! Leave!" I hiss at the Masca, who is thoroughly enjoying worrying at Freddy's limp arm. He gives it a further enthusiastic tug then, with a growl, lets go. "Right, this fucker must have some sort of hall pass on him." I say out loud to Fitz who chuckles in response.

The last thing I want to do is frisk the alien, so I half close my eyes and run my hands over his clothing and down each arm. On one wrist there is clipped a bracelet that has to be the way he gains entry around the ship. It's worth a try. I pull it off him and then contemplate the body. If he wakes up, he's going to raise the alarm and I need as long as possible to find Rex. I push him to the top of the bed and then roll him down, wrapping him in the sheets as tightly as I can.

I press the bracelet thing on a black pad next to the door and it slides open. Peering out into the corridor, I'm pleased to find it empty of any Grolix.

"Fitz?" I look down at the little Masca. He's still not quite returned to his sleek form after the fight with Freddy and remains fizzing with energy.

I take a deep breath and head into the Grolix ship, back the way I came, hoping I can find Rex before they find I'm missing.

36

REX

I'm lying in a puddle of liquid. From the smell, I don't even want to hazard a guess at what it is. Every muscle in my body is screaming at me and I remember being repeatedly shocked as Jayne looked on.

I have failed my mate like I failed my brave warriors on that ill-fated mission. I planned for our discovery, just not on Katahrr. I thought that we would make it off world before they found us. Now Jayne's at risk along with my unborn child. It's enough to get me heaving myself to my feet and checking my surroundings. The dank cell is lit by a single grill in the roof and it looks like that is the only way in or out. I jump up to grab the bars and I'm shocked again by the collar around my neck. There's less force this time, more of a warning to behave. I slump down against one dirty wall and contemplate my next move.

At least we have left Katharr. As long as we're on the move there is a chance. My only problem is how to get out of the cell and free of this collar. Should be easy for a warrior of my experience.

I'm gingerly exploring the mechanics of the shock collar when a familiar snuffling sound above me attracts my attention. Looking up, I see the squat, blunt head of Fitz, his red eyes staring down at me.

"Fitz!" I never thought I'd be pleased to see the creature, but right now, I think he's what I need. "Come on boy!" I call out, tapping my hand on my lap to try and entice him down.

"Rex?" Jayne's face appears at the bars, and I'm immediately on my feet, wanting to reach for her and knowing I risk a shock if I do.

"What are you doing here?" I hiss, "If they find you, they will punish you."

"I doubt that very much," she says, kneeling next to the opening. She looks pale although there are two bright spots on her cheeks. "The Grolix need me for something and they don't dare touch me. How do I get you out?" She reaches for the bars and pulls at them. They swing upwards, and she drops the hatch with a loud clang.

"Shit!" She exclaims, looking wildly behind her. "I thought it would be locked."

"It doesn't need to be," I point at my collar. "This is programmed to stun me if I try and get out."

"For fuck's sake! Isn't anything in this galaxy easy?" Jayne swears in exasperation.

"I think I can get out of it. Can you send Fitz down?"

Jayne looks at me quizzically before calling the Masca over and encouraging him to drop into my cell.

"How do I make him do the sparking thing?" I call up to Jayne.

"You want him to do that?" She stares down at me, and I notice her eyes are fever bright with fear. "Just touch him on the very top of his head, for some reason he hates being touched there." She looks around herself wildly again.

I encourage Fitz to settle around my neck, like he does around Jayne's, uttering soothing noises until he is happily ensconced. I tickle behind his ears and move my hand up to the top of his head, giving him a hard pat. He responds instantaneously with a yowl and several sharp cracks of electricity, each one more painful than the last before he swarms off me and leaps out of the cell into Jayne's arms, chittering noisily in disgust.

The control collar gives a soft chime and falls away. I reach for the opening above me and pull myself out. It's only when I'm clear of the dank hole that I hear Jayne's laughter.

"Oh my God, Rex! Your face when Fitz went off!" She giggles.

Her laughter has a slight edge to it that I like even less than the pallor to her skin. I gather her and the creature in my arms and hold her close. She's trembling.

"Are you okay, my mate?" I ask her, brushing her hair away from her face.

"I'm fine." She says bravely, "just outside my comfort zone with all this alien kidnapping stuff. How do we get off this fucking ship?"

"We need to get to an escape pod, then I've arranged a rendezvous with some friends." I explain as I help her to her feet. To my relief, she smiles, and her whole face lights up.

With Jayne's hand clutched tightly in mine, we venture out into the ship. If my reading of the Grolix schematics is correct, we will have to go up two levels to get to the escape pods. I spot what I need, the internal ducting hatch.

"Keep a look out, *kedves*. I need to get this off." I start to pry at the surrounding bolts, digging my claws into the metal.

"Would this help?" Jayne holds out a keybracelet.

"Where did you get this?"

"I'll tell you later. I think I can hear someone coming!" Jayne hisses.

The keybraclelet chimes, and the hatch swings open. I help Jayne into the ducting first then follow, squeezing myself through the too small opening.

'Can you climb?" I point upwards, whilst staring at her rounded stomach.

Jayne huffs out a breath at me and starts to scramble up the inside of the ducting with remarkable ease. So much so, I have to work quite hard to catch up with her.

'We're heading for that hatch, just above you." I call out to make sure she doesn't climb past it.

Jayne halts next to the hatch and waits for me to reach her, looking completely at home hanging from the various wires and tubes that we have used in our climb.

"What?" She asks as I capture her lips in an impromptu kiss. "I've always loved to climb. It was one of the only things I did when I wasn't working. Stop being soppy and get us out of here, Mr Warrior!"

Honestly, if we hadn't been dangling sixty foot up in this ducting, I would've fucked my delectable mate there and then. Instead, I remind my cock that there is plenty of time for that in our future and release the catch on the hatch. A quick check shows me that the surrounding area is free of Grolix, and having helped Jayne out of the ducting, I quickly follow her. Fitz appears at her feet, humming and chuckling to himself. It doesn't look like he has forgiven me for using him to get free of the control collar as he gives me a side eye a lesser creature might fear.

I take Jayne's hand again and she sticks close behind me as we carefully make our way towards the escape pods. We are almost at the pod dock when I hear a sound behind us. The sound of a pair of clapping hands.

"Well done, Haalux, you got further than I thought you would," Hardag's voice rings out.

I tuck Jayne behind me as I turn to face the massive Grolix and his followers.

"This is between me and you, Hardag. Let the female go." I growl.

"On the contrary, we don't really need you. Our job was for the female only. My allies wanted a human female for impregnation, and now you've done the job for them. So hand her over and you can go."

"Not a chance, Hardag. If you want her, you'll have to go through me." I snarl. Red mounts in my vision. This disgusting Grolix has already tried to take my mate once. He's not doing it again. I move into a fighting stance and beckon to him.

Hardag squares his shoulders and puts out his enormous arms to shove back the Grolix warriors jostling behind him, then he starts to pound across the deck towards me with a roar.

37

JAYNE

Rex shoves me to one side as Hardag throws himself across the room. He plunges head first at the Grolix, who is hell bent on tearing Rex limb from limb. My warrior roars, and they hit each other in a cringingly loud crunch of muscle. I back away into a corner as Hardag manages to get his arms around Rex's waist and tries to flip him. He uses his sharp tusks to gouge at Rex's flesh, and I cry out as the wounds start to flow with bright red blood.

Rex looks over at me and that breaks his concentration, allowing Hardag to dump him on his back. Rex recovers quickly and plants a heavy boot in Hardag's stomach, throwing the big Grolix back to sprawl on his behind. With a suppleness that his huge form didn't appear to have, Hardag flips himself upright and advances on Rex with murder in his eyes. As he has his back to me, I can see the knife that is attached to his waistband.

"Rex!" I shout out to warn him.

Rex has already seen the flash of the blade and jumps clear as Hardag swings for him. The knife just catches his abdomen and a streak of red appears. Rex roars out in fury and lunges for Hardag, claws outstretched. The knife skitters across the floor as Hardag goes down, hard, with Rex on top of him. Rex beats at his head, claws hitting home each time. Hardag wriggles under him and I see his warriors start to move towards the fighting pair, until he yells out for them to stay back.

With a tremendous effort, Hardag gets clear of Rex's claws and manages to slide his way over to the knife. He gets to his feet, his chest heaving with the effort, his skin streaked with black-green blood. He beckons at Rex, who, although he's injured, still looks fresh. Hardag looks over at me and cups his crotch through his loincloth. The gesture instantly causes Rex to charge him. He hits Hardag hard on one side and the pair of them tumble over and over, just as the entire ship lurches to one side.

It looks like the attackers have become the attacked. I scramble to grab onto to something to avoid sliding towards the fight and to Hardag's warriors, although I note with some satisfaction that they have diminished in numbers when the ship started to shift. There is a blinding flash of light and I turn my face away, eyes tight shut, expecting at any minute to be sucked into the vacuum of space. I hear Rex and Hardag still fighting as the deck shakes under me. There is a burst of blaster fire and a heavy hand hits my shoulder, jolting me into action.

I leap up, ready to fight my attacker as best I can, but as I get to my feet I see the retreating back of Hardag and Rex's prone body.

"No!" I twist away from whoever is holding me and fly across the room to Rex. Hardag's knife is buried in his side and he groans.

"I'm here, Rex!" I hold his head and press a kiss to his lips.

"*Kedves*, my mate." He looks blearily up at me and tries to sit up. I push him down, "Don't move! I'll get help."

Finally, I look around me. We're surrounded by warriors, Haalux warriors. Armed to the teeth and dressed like Rex, my mouth falls open as I take in the sight. One large warrior steps forward. A long scar from his forehead to his chin marrs his Hallan marking.

"I'm Bron, Captain of the *Freebird*. If you'll let our brother go, I can promise we will help him."

All of the warriors bow their heads. Rex moans quietly.

"Please, please help him! Rex is my mate and I'm carrying his child." I hear myself saying, one hand on Rex's bloody chest and one on my stomach.

Bron helps me to my feet, and his warriors swarm in to lift Rex easily. They carry him towards a large hole that has been made in the side of the ship.

"If you will join me, mate of Commander Rexitor, I would welcome your presence on my ship, before I blow this one to atoms." He grins a lopsided grin at me.

Captain Bron doesn't need to ask twice. I'm already hurrying through the hole and following the warriors carrying Rex. Behind me, I hear the sound of an airlock closing and the *Freebird* rocks slightly as we disengage from the Grolix ship. With Rex in my sights, I ignore anything else until we reach a med bay with a familiar medic waiting for us.

"Jaal?" I cry out. My legs buckle at the sight of a recognizable face. He takes a few steps to catch me. "Never mind me! Rex is hurt! Please help Rex!" I yell at him, just as everything goes dark.

38

REX

A pair of red eyes stare down at me, and for a moment I think it's Fitz, until my eyes focus properly on the face of Jaal.

"What the-?" I struggle to sit. My side burns where Hardag managed to drive the blade, before the coward ran from the sight of my Haalux brothers. Jaal hoists me into a sitting position with little regard to my pain levels. Nothing changed there. "What are you doing here, Jaal? And where is here? Where is my mate?" The questions spill out of me.

I remember seeing other Haalux warriors and Jayne's worried face, then nothing. I go to get out of the pod. I need to get to Jayne.

"Woah! Easy there, warrior. Take your time. Jayne is absolutely fine, as is your child. I sent her to get some food. She hasn't left your side with that dratted creature since you were brought in." Jaal pushes me gently back into the pod and I relax a little. "You are on Captain Bron's ship, *Freebird*, a Hunter-Class craft. As to my being here, that's a longer story."

"*Captain* Bron?" The only Haalux I know called Bron was my second in command. An exceptional and brave warrior who perished due to my negligence on the mission to free the Council member's son from the slavers.

"Did you not think I could make it to Captain, Commander?" I look across the med bay to see the source of the voice I recognize but never thought I'd hear again.

"Bron?" The Haalux warrior that strides towards my pod is alive and well. His perfect Hallan marred by a terrible scar that runs the full length of his face. "I thought you dead, brother." My voice cracks.

"As I did you, my brother." Bron grasps my arm in our old greeting. "I thought all of our team dead, so many were atomized."

"But I saw you, the laser cannon cut you down..." I know I'm staring at Bron like he is a ghost. To me, he is. No one could have survived that place. I barely got out alive with our target.

"Just a few flesh wounds," Bron laughs and runs his hand over his damaged face. "Nothing that didn't heal with the time I spent at the hands of that bastard, Hardag."

"Hardag ran the slave planet?"

"He's not going to be running anything much longer if I get a say in it," Bron says, darkly. "It is good to see you, alive and well, Rex." He grins at me. "And with such a pretty mate in tow. You've been busy."

"Jayne!" My thoughts immediately jump back to her, even with the enormity of finding Bron alive. I struggle to get out of the pod and Jaal goes to push me back again.

"Let me take him to his mate, Jaal. You know the only other way you'll keep him here is by sedating him." Bron says to the fussing medic and helps me out of the pod.

"I'd like to see you try that, Jaal." I growl back at him as he carefully puts the hypo he just picked up down.

"Just take it easy, Commander," He grumbles. "And tell your wayward mate I need her to come back for a check-up. She can leave the Masca elsewhere."

"What's been going on?" I ask Bron as he lets me lean on him for my first few steps, "Other than you coming back from the dead,"

"Both of us, Rex," Bron laughs and I realize I've missed hearing his laugh almost as much as I beat myself up about losing him and my team.

"I mean, Forat promised me he would organize transport back to

Haalux once I had found Jayne, so that I could address the Council, but I never expected it to be a Fleet Hunter-Class doing the transporting. Not unless I was to be dragged before them in chains."

"Ah, well, about that Rex—" Bron begins to speak as we enter the canteen.

My eyes lock on my mate. She has cleansed, her long flaming hair cascading over her shoulders. She is dressed in figure hugging clothing that emphasise both her delicious breasts and glorious rounded pregnancy. She sits at a table eating a bowl of *Djelin*, and laughing at Fitz, who is engaged in a standoff with a couple of young Haalux warriors.

The silly creature alternates between being a ball of spikes and electricity to his sleek form each time the warriors toss him some food. Jayne's eyes meet mine and it is like time stands still, except that she ends up in my arms, her ripe little body entwined with mine, her lips heating my rogue Hallan. I lose myself in her embrace, in her form and I remember my promise to myself when we were climbing the ducting.

"Where are our quarters?" I release her just long enough to growl my question at Bron.

He gives me his best knowing grin and gestures for me to follow him. I toss Jayne into my arms, and she doesn't make a sound, simply nuzzling along my jawline in a way that has my cock pressing painfully at my trousers and I'm willing Bron to move faster.

"You're in here," Bron finally stops outside a cabin door. "I guess I'll see you when I see you. You know where to find me." He chuckles as the door slides open and I stride in.

The cabin is very similar to mine on *Excelsior* and Jayne has noticed too as she wriggles to be let down. As soon as she is on her feet, her hands are worrying at my clothing, pulling to free my throbbing cock.

"I thought I'd lost you, Rex," She grips my length with both hands, running delicious strokes up and over my sensitive head. "I never want to lose you again."

"It takes more than a little fight to keep me from you, *kedves*." I murmur, my voice hoarse at her touch.

I strip away her clothing until she is bare before me. It is only when she lies back on the bed enticing and wanton, I remember that, finally, we have all the time we need.

I'm going to take this very slow, whether she wants me to or not.

39

JAYNE

As soon as I saw Rex standing in the doorway of the canteen, something inside me flipped. The warmth that spreads through me, morphing into desire when he strides across the room, so full of life, healthy and handsome to take me in his strong arms. When he was lying in the med bay, his Hallan dulled as he fought his way back from injury, I knew there was something between us, and it was more than just our want for each other and the child that grows within me.

My training as a lawyer taught me how to hide my emotions. Being able to maintain a 'poker face' is a tactic that always came in handy, whether it was to avoid betraying my concerns to my opponent in the court room or keeping a straight face whilst a client spun me a tale, I believe I excelled in maintaining a calm and controlled demeanor. I was so good, I could even keep my emotions from myself. I had given up on ever finding love, of being able to let someone into my tightly maintained life. I think I had even decided I was better off on my own.

When my world fell apart, I only had myself to blame. Why not wallow in my own misfortune? It wasn't as if my parents had cared much. My career was everything to them. I lost anything that they might have considered to be love when that went down the toilet. From success to instant disappointment.

But Rex doesn't see me like that. All he sees is me, his fated mate. It was complicated for him, but now he's embraced me as his mate, something his species are predisposed to have, it's become simple for him. The only thing holding me back is whether being his mate is the same as being in love. I don't know if he loves me or if he is just giving into his genetics.

He wants me. I can feel it in the hard rod pressing against my bottom as he picks me up and demands to be taken to our quarters. I have to learn how to let go of my past and move on, because I want him more than anything as he strips me naked and his heated orange gaze runs over my plump body.

"You are so beautiful, my mate," He breathes as he moves, predatorily, up the bed over me. "And you get more beautiful every time I look at you." He runs his hands over my bump and to my heavy breasts, his thumbs brushing over my raised nipples.

He mounts me, his muscular bulk enclosing me as he kisses down my neck towards my tight peaks, one of which he captures in his lips, circling and sucking on the hard nub. He teases me into a moan of pleasure as I arc my back upwards towards him. Rex descends, gently parting my thighs. He stares intently at me as his thumb finds my clit and applies just the right amount of pressure, making me buck at him.

"Not so fast, *kedves*," Rex growls and slips a thick digit inside me, letting out a groan as he finds me wet and willing for him.

He lowers his head and buries it between my legs, his Hallan on his lips sparking over my clit as he laps at me, his tongue exploring my folds, dipping inside me as his lips vibrate deliciously over my nub. I grab at his head, my fingers entwining in his hair as I urge him on. Rex raises his head, his chin covered in my juices, grinning wildly that I'm enjoying his attentions, and I push him back down as he chuckles, redoubling his efforts over my clit, nipping at me with his sharp teeth. He pulls my clit into his mouth and sucks hard, at the same time inserting his fingers deep into me, pumping at my soaking pussy. My threatening orgasm overwhelms me. I convulse against him, moisture flooding his fingers and lapping tongue and, he groans in ecstasy.

I want him inside me, to bring me to even more climaxes, and to his surprise, I roll onto my rounded stomach, slowly lifting my bottom up as I raise myself onto my hands and knees. I look over my shoulder to see Rex looking both highly aroused and confused, his thick cock hard up against his muscular stomach. I wriggle my bum at him.

"Take me, Rex." I breathe.

He doesn't need asking twice, he grabs at my hips and his member notches at my entrance, wet and ready for him. He lets out a long moan as he pushes inside me, my earlier orgasm easing the way for his huge shaft to fill me to my core. His hand caresses my rounded belly, searching for my clit. He begins to thrust, slowly at first, letting me get used to his size, even though his labored breathing indicates he's struggling to hold back. With each thrust he presses on my clit, and I get wetter for him until he loses his control, pounding me hard from behind, withdrawing almost all the way before he drives back into me. With every stroke, his Hallan heats me, the hot marking dragging over my G-spot and bringing me closer and closer to my second climax. Rex has a firm hold of my buttocks, and as I look back at him, he opens his eyes.

"I can't - I can't" He pants out, his skin shining with sweat, and I feel him explode inside me, each irregular pump firing more of his hot spicy seed. My climax is swift and devastating as I buck and writhe in Rex's grasp. He holds me to him, his cock buried deep and one arm around my waist. I feel his hard chest over my back as he recovers his breath, until he eventually rolls onto the bed, taking me with him.

"Wicked mate," He says in my ear, his lips brushing me, "I wanted to take things slow and you drove me wild."

"I never want you to take me slow," I laugh, "I always want you hard and fast." Rex's arm is curled over my burgeoning bump, and he caresses it with a touch so tender, it almost makes me want to cry.

We're safe. We've got so much to discuss, but for now, I want to lose myself in my gorgeous Rex and forget it all for a while.

40

REX

J ayne cuddles up to me, her face sleepy and satisfied. I should be the one who's tired. She has taken me again and again, insatiably, and I love her for it. I wrap my arms around her sweet, plump form, filled with my child.

"Are you happy, my mate?"

Jayne hums with pleasure as she snuggles further into my arms. That she takes pleasure in me is wonderful, but I'm still not sure if humans mate in the same way as Haalux. She knows I will not leave her, that I will always come for her. I just need to know that she feels the same way too. I presume that she will tell me in time.

Somewhere in our quarters there is a soft chime of a comm. I want to ignore it and spend more time in Jayne's arms, but I know we can't avoid the rest of the ship, and I need to speak further with Bron. The sound comes again, and with a sigh, I move out from under Jayne's soft body to reach the comm on the wall.

"Yes?"

"I need to check you and your mate." Of course it's Jaal interrupting us. "And Bron needs to debrief you."

"We'll be along shortly," I grunt into the comm before turning it off.

Jayne stretches out luxuriously on the bed. "How long is shortly?" She asks with a heated gaze aimed directly at my cock.

Some considerable time later, we arrive in Jaal's med bay. He gives us both a knowing look, which Jayne returns cooly.

"Don't even try that one, Jaal. I'm only speaking to you because you helped Rex." She says to him.

I give her a quizzical look.

"Jaal apparently accidentally removed my birth control when we were on the *Excelsior*." Jayne folds her arms and taps her foot, her pregnancy protruding in her skintight suit.

"Do you not want to have my child?" I ask her, breaking her staring contest with Jaal, my heart skipping a beat.

She immediately has her arms around me, her face upturned to mine, blue eyes shining. "Oh no, Rex, please don't think that. I—" She hesitates for a fraction of a second, "I care for you very much and I want to have your baby, our baby." She takes my hand and places it on her stomach. "You're the best thing that ever happened to me." She whispers, and my heart rate returns to near normal.

"I'm annoyed with Jaal because what he did was reckless with my health and our baby's health." She's turned back to Jaal and is giving him the full benefit of her steely gaze. "I'm an older mother by human standards and that can carry risks for the child, plus he had no idea what the risks of a human/Haalux mating would produce, given that Haalux don't mate outside their own kind."

I can see how she would be fearsome in the human courtroom she described to me as her words bear down on the medic. Jaal would have retreated further, had his back not been already up against the wall of the med bay.

"That's not entirely the case, Jayne." I say, gently. "There are other Haalux males that have fathered half-Haalux with other species, my friend Forat for one."

Jayne is still obviously not impressed. Her eyes narrow at Jaal. "Is this true?"

"It is, sweet one. And you know I always had your best interests at heart." Jaal tries, with a smile on his face the like of which I've never seen before.

Fitz pops into existence next to her, and Jaal recoils as the Masca swarms up her to settle around her neck, chuckling to himself. "I can't have that thing in my med bay." He spits out.

"Fitz isn't going anywhere! Get used to it!" Jayne says, firmly. "Are you going to check Rex or what?"

Jaal gives a snort of annoyance but inclines his head at me. Jayne watches with interest as I peel off my top to present my wound to Jaal.

"Healing well, as expected. You're fine." He says dismissively, then looks expectantly at Jayne.

She huffs a breath and settles herself into a pod, arms still crossed over her ample chest. Jaal produces a holo-screen and punches at it for a long few moments, until Jayne is leaning forward.

"Is everything okay?" She asks, a hit of concern in her voice. I've known Jaal long enough to see he's playing her, but I want her to forgive him so I say nothing.

"Everything is fine." He eventually says. "Mother and baby are doing very well." He beams at me and I hop onto the pod beside my gorgeous, pouting mate, dislodging Fitz. The creature hisses at me as I cuddle up to her.

"That's good to hear. No more excitement for my mate. Just plenty of time to rest and grow this little one." I smooth over her rounded belly, and she smiles up at me, her blue eyes twinkling.

I need to buy her some *bilik* jewels to match them, and to thank her for giving me everything I never thought I would have.

'Well, well, Commander Rexitor, the mated male." Bron laughs as he enters the med bay.

I make a show of being comfortable in the pod and give Bron a shit-eating grin, Jayne snuggled at my side. I'm not in any way insulted by the idea of being a mated male, quite the contrary and it's very pleasant.

"Captain Bron, back from the dead," I reply.

"You need to debrief," Bron says to me. He's all seriousness, reminiscent of our days together on our old vessel with our old crew.

"Yes, I do," I kiss Jayne on the top of her head, "I'll be back, try not to give Jaal too hard a time."

"What we need to discuss concerns your mate too, Rex." Bron says, inclining his head at Jayne.

"No rest for the wicked," Jayne follows me out of the pod.

We wind our way through the ship until we reach Bron's ready room. There are two other Haalux warriors already waiting for us. Bron introduces them as his second in command, Jak and his head of security, Terx. They are big, strong warriors, but their faces soften when they see Jayne follow me in. Terx clucks his tongue at Fitz and, to my surprise, the Masca flows over to him immediately, swarming into his arms. He ruffs up Fitz's fur as he settles back in his chair.

"Commander Terx has a way with lesser lifeforms," Bron says, seeing my gaze. I grunt in return, and Jayne giggles at me. I may have to re-evaluate the mated male situation.

Jayne sits down, and Fitz whizzes over to her, chirping as he settles around her neck.

"Did you get Hardag?" I ask, still not sure exactly what happened after the bastard stuck me with his blade.

"No, he managed to hyper-jump before we could get a torpedo-bolt off at his ship." Bron grinds out, clearly not happy that the slaver got away.

"We've got his engine signature and hopefully will pick him up at some point," Jak says quietly. He's an intense looking Haalux with perfect Hallan. There's an air of quiet confidence about him that makes me keen to have him on my team. A perfect warrior.

"As much as I hate to admit it, Hardag can wait," Bron's eyes blaze. "Our mission is to get Rex and Jayne back to Haalux."

"It is?" Jayne chimes in, making all the males in the room look at her and putting me entirely on edge. "I'd have thought that's the last place that either of us should be going. I'm a wanted criminal and Rex is accused of helping me." She raises her eyebrows, her blue eyes piercing as she strokes Fitz.

Bron gives the other warriors a look that I can't quite fathom.

"There's been something wrong at the heart of the Empire for some time, Rex. Having spent enforced time out of the Fleet and the Empire, when I finally got back, I noticed it immediately," Bron leans forward, "I think you were specifically kept away from the heart of things, Rex, once you had returned the Council member's son to Haalux. That's why you ended up on the *Excelsior* at the opposite end of the Galaxy."

"Why? I've done my duty for the Empire. I lost everything in that last mission, present company excepted, Bron. I'm a warrior with something to prove, but that's only because of this." I run my finger over my rogue Hallan.

"Rather like me, your contact with the slave planet marked you out more than you realize," Bron says, contemplatively. "What I saw in my time there was enough to persuade a couple of the more senior Captains in the fleet to take action, which is why I got command of the *Freebird*. That included Captain Clarin." Bron nodded towards me. "I'm sorry, Rex, I had to ask him to keep my return from you. It was essential, initially, that we went under the radar, and I know you would have requested to join me if you had known."

Although I'm not happy that any of this has been kept from me, I understand why Bron did it. It also goes a long way to explaining Captain Clarin's behavior on the *Excelsior* and how I made my escape.

"The Empire has a new enemy, Rex. Whoever they are, they have managed to get right to the heart," Bron says, grimly.

"Whoever they are? You mean The Unseen?" I say and Bron starts in surprise. "I came across mention of them when I was looking for Jayne after the Grolix took her. But that's all they were, words. No descriptions and nothing tangible."

"That's the problem. No one knows who they are. Where we come into contact with those who have done their business, all we get told is that they are known as 'The Unseen'. Either they are able to change their appearance at will or are able to completely disguise themselves. There's no way of knowing."

"So we're looking for an invisible enemy, somewhere in the Galaxy, who may or may not have infiltrated the highest echelons of Haalux power?" Jayne asks, quietly.

Bron lets out a long breath. "When you put it like that…"

"I presume you have more than circumstantial evidence." Jayne adds, her eyes not leaving Bron for an instant.

"Hardag was involved in transporting weapons and other supplies to various asteroid-stations. He was also the go-between for The Unseen and the Grolix they hired to do their dirty work. We've been working hard to try and identify who he was in contact with in order to determine who, within the Empire, has been influenced by The Unseen,"

"And?" My mate is not letting Bron off the hook for a second.

"Ambassador Roi was a double agent. The Unseen killed him for it and chose to spread further confusion by placing the blame on you." Bron says.

Jayne's intake of breath is audible. She sits back in her chair, wrapping her arms around herself.

"It would have caused too much interest on the wrong Haalux if the killing had been perpetrated by a Haalux or one of our allies. Using a primitive species was a calculated risk for them." Bron bows his head at Jayne, "I think they underestimated you."

"You were aware of the trial?" I ask.

"Following avidly, Brother. Forat made sure of it."

"Forat's involved in this too?" I shouldn't be surprised. That old privateer would always have his hand in if he thought he could turn a profit.

"You can see why we need to return to Haalux. The best way to clear you both is to go to the center and take out the rotten core." Bron explains. "The *Freebird* has been operating on the periphery of the Fleet for some time. We should easily be able to get into Haalux space. Once we are in, I've got contacts on Haalux that mean we should be able to land."

"And then what?"

"We've got to get to the Council and confront them with the evidence."

"Just that?" I snort with laughter. "I thought we were going to have to do something dangerous."

"It'll be just like Aros Prime, brother." Bron matches my laughter and gets up from his chair, striding over to me, he grasps my forearm. "I've been waiting a long time to be back fighting by your side, Rex. I know we can do this, for you, your mate, and the Empire."

"Aros Prime was a shit-show," I grin back at him. "And I'm up for anything like that whole bunch of fun."

"Set course for Haalux and ready the warriors," Bron says to Jak, who heads through to the bridge. "We'll need to brief our contacts." He says to Terx. The taciturn warrior nods and follows Jak.

"When you are quite done with your testosterone-fest, great warrior, your mate would like some breakfast now." Jayne says, drawing my attention to her. Fitz crackles as if in agreement.

"There's no way I'm going to disagree with your mate," Bron stands away, hands held high. "The canteen's at your disposal, sweet female."

41

JAYNE

I'm absolutely starving, although I'm pleased that Rex included me in the briefing they had. I'm thinking over what Bron said as I walk with Rex through the ship to the canteen.

"Are you nervous, my *kedves*?" Rex asks as we enter the canteen, which is relatively empty of Haalux warriors.

Whilst it's a good feeling to be on a Haalux ship and to not be a prisoner, some of the younger warriors are rather too fascinated by me. I'm guessing that they have not been through a Zycle and are unused to seeing a pregnant female. Their staring has been a little unnerving.

"I guess I am nervous, a bit. I can't help but wonder if we're walking into a trap of some sort." Along with everything else unpleasant that could happen to me. "Your friend seems confident in his information though."

I take a seat in the canteen, and Rex slides in opposite me. He fixes me with his deep orange eyes.

"Bron is one of my oldest comrades. He is a warrior beyond compare. I trust him with my life." He says with some feeling.

"Except he deliberately kept the fact he was alive from you."

Rex contemplates me for a while. "No, that's true." He drops his gaze, and I feel horrible that I'm casting doubt on a friendship that clearly goes back a long way.

"Don't mind me, Rex. I have trust issues, you know that. I'm sure it'll all be fine." I say. I'm hungry and tired after all our activities last night, and my stomach takes the opportunity to let out a growl, surprising Fitz, who spikes and crackles. "Any chance of something to eat?"

Rex springs up and heads over to the counter. After a discussion with the Haalux in their version of a kitchen, resembling a cross between a laboratory and an airplane galley, he returns with a tray of food, which he places in front of me with a flourish. I recognize the strange blue soup that I've been mostly eating over the past few days whilst Rex recovered in the med bay, but some of the other things I've never seen before.

"That's *Djelin*," He explains pointing to the soup, "and these are *ovo*," Rex picks up one of the round pink things and takes a bite before offering it to me.

I nibble at it, it tastes like a sweet, steamed bun, and I devour the rest before getting stuck into the incredibly tasty soup, all spicy and hot, a bit like the handsome Haalux Commander sitting opposite me. *My mate*. I remind myself. Still an alien concept I'm not entirely sure about. I wish I could pin down my feelings about Rex. When I was on Katahrr he was all I could think about, when Hardag stabbed him, I thought my world had fallen apart. But when he sits opposite me, looking muscular, gorgeous and noble, my stomach squirms. I want to tell him how I feel, or at least that I don't know what to feel, but my words dry up.

Not something that used to be a problem. Words were my business, I made them work for me. I crafted statements, twisted the words of others to suit my needs. Yet, when I really need them, when they actually matter to me, they are like smoke. I can't capture them in the same way Rex has captured me.

"I trust Bron with my life and yours," He says, his face a mask of seriousness. "He was my second in command when I commanded a Hunter-Class vessel like this one. Our team had a reputation for being a surgical instrument when it came to infiltration missions. It's why we were chosen to go to Lyra to free the Council Member's son." He hesitates, "I'm wondering if even that mission was a set up."

Rex's eyes darken, and I get it. The Empire is everything to these warriors and there's nothing wrong with that, except when it's challenged.

"What we found on Lyra was nothing like we were led to believe, especially the resistance. My team, Bron. I thought I had lost them all." His voice is low as his head dips.

I place my hand over his on the table.

"If you trust Bron, then I trust him," I squeeze at his muscular fingers. "None of this is easy on you or your friends. I understand what it means to have your whole world change in an instant. At least you were not at fault."

"Maybe I am," Rex's eyes are full of pain when he looks up at me. "Maybe I should have questioned more after I lost Bron and my men, it's just..." He tails off and looks over my head at the wall.

"Rex," I say softly to bring his attention back to me, "it's not your fault. Someone once told me that no one knows everything."

Rex lifts his head to look at me and a smile appears, the one I once vowed to myself I wanted to make sure stayed on his face. It warms my heart and heats my core.

"I wonder who was the brave and intelligent being who said that." His smile has turned into a rather smug grin.

I pick up the last remaining *ovo* and with a flick of my wrist, I hit him directly in his eye. The soft bun sticks and then slowly slides off.

"You, little human, are going to pay for that." Rex growls as he wipes away the remains of the bun from his face.

"What are you gonna do about it?" I giggle at him.

In a flash, Rex has me in his arms and is striding out of the canteen with the shocked stares of the younger crew members following us as I squeal, and he growls his way to our quarters.

42

REX

I leave Jayne sleeping soundly, Fitz curled at her side. Whatever I do, I can't seem to keep the creature out of our quarters, and I've stopped trying. I envy her deep sleep. She did her best to relax me, but it looks like the worn out one is her.

Bron is on the bridge as I enter. I wait for him to motion me in. This is his ship. I'm proud that he made captain. He was a good officer and deserved the promotion, far more than I ever did.

"We've just entered Haalux space," Bron says. The bridge is in semi-darkness.

"You're using a stealth-screen?" I ask. It's not normally installed on Haalux vessels.

Bron reads my mind. "Had it retrofitted a while back. I resisted for a while, but with what we have been doing, it made sense."

I stare out towards Haalux. The red glow of the lesser sun and the brightness of the mother sun illuminate the planet as we travel towards it.

"I'd have thought we'd have to drag you away from your mate, not that you'd leave her voluntarily." Bron grins at me.

"Believe me, if I could spend every moment inside her, I would." I grin back at Bron. As far as I was aware, he's not had a Zycle yet, and that's one thing I have over him. "She needs to rest though."

Bron lets out a bark of laughter and claps me on the shoulder. "More to this mating lark than meets the eye, eh?"

"It's good, Bron. You should try it some time." I grin at him. "What are we walking into on Haalux?" He is immediately serious and flings himself back in his chair.

"This new enemy is extremely dangerous. From all reports they are vicious and will stop at nothing to get to their end goal. They terrify all lesser life forms that they force to join their cause."

"Is that really that much different to how the Empire set out?" I lean back on a console.

"As far as I'm aware, impressive though the Empire was, is, we never caused any species to take its own life rather than reveal it's sources. Any worlds we conquered were always give a choice and benefitted from our patronage. You know that as well as I do, brother." Bron says.

I nod in agreement. Our approach was to always conquer, protect and benefit from the planets we adopted into the Empire.

"This Unseen, they remind me of the Xarax," I'm thinking out loud. Bron huffs out an angry breath and a number of warriors look up from their work at the sound of our old enemy's name. "They expected death everywhere they went."

"The Xarax have not been seen in this Galaxy for many, many turns, Rex." Bron says loudly for the benefit of his crew. "The last that was heard of them was that a great plague had wiped them from the face of their home world. Those who visited told of a broken planet and what little of the Xarax remained were a shadow of their former selves."

"That's not saying much, they were disgusting creatures." I snort. Unlike Bron, I was in the last wave to fight against them. I can still hear the sound of their clicking mandibles in my darkest nightmares.

"They're gone, Rex, and we have to convince enough of Haalux high command that the Unseen are as big a threat." Bron says.

"Come, old friend, we're not due to land for another few hours, come and have a drink with me."

He jumps to his feet and leads me from the bridge to his ready room, where he pulls out a bottle of *Per*.

"I've been saving this for some time, for a special occasion. I think that toasting our reunion and your successful mating is as good an occasion as any." He pours out two large measures of the deep purple liquor.

"To us, the warriors, and the Empire." I make the traditional toast, the one we always used to make before a mission.

"To you, Rex, and your future." Bron responds before tossing back his glass in one gulp. He has a twinkle in his eye that suggests this might end up being a long night.

I crawl back into my quarters sometime later and only after Bron and I had helped each other stagger back to the accommodation area. Jayne uncurls herself and snuggles against me, soft, warm, and fragrant.

"Uhg!" She announces, her sweet little nose wrinkling delightfully, "what have you been doing?"

"Jus' a sparring match with my brother an' a few drinks." I'm slurring my words.

"You stink, Rex, bugger off." She pushes at me, but I'm not moving. I'm not sure I can. The whole place is spinning and our impromptu training session was no holds barred.

"Stupid male." She says sleepily before she curls up against me and falls back asleep. It's not long before I follow her.

When I wake, it's to the piercing sound of the comm. I stumble out of bed, cursing Bron and his *Per*, to stop the noise.

"We'll be landing on Haalux in an hour, Commander" Terx voice announces to me.

"Tell your Captain I want a rematch." I say, my voice gravelly. "And have you seen my mate?"

"She's on the bridge with us," Terx replies and terminates the comm.

That's more than enough to have me searching for my clothing and getting ready in double time. I stroll onto the bridge, trying to look as cool as possible. Jayne sits at a console with a rather nervous looking young warrior showing her the controls. Fitz is settled at her feet, slightly spiky as he watches every move the warrior makes. I try not to smile at the creature, protecting its mistress.

"Rex!" Bron stands and clasps my arm. "We've been given clearance to land and will start the protocol shortly."

"Where is the landing site?" I ask as Jayne leaves the console and walks over to join us.

She looks particularly delicious, and I regret my night time session with Bron meant I missed enjoying her ripe body this morning.

"You're up then?" She smiles at me, although there's something in her eyes that makes me think we have unfinished business that isn't the pleasure I'm imagining. "I've already had words with your *brother* about last night. Not impressed." She shoots Bron a look, and he holds up his hands, laughing.

"Dearest, I promise I will not lead your mate astray again." He says as I bristle at him calling her 'dearest'.

"I can promise you a world of hurt if you do, *Captain*." Jayne says, sweetly as she reaches forward and grabs his crotch, giving it a hard twist and then letting go so quickly I'm not entirely sure what I have seen.

Bron stumbles back, his hands covering his cock as he lets out a high-pitched whine, desperate not to let his men see what the tiny female has done to him. Jak and Terx look in different directions, trying not to smile. Jayne looks very satisfied at the havoc she's caused and turns to me, prodding me in my chest.

"Not impressed at all, Rex. I'm going to get something to eat before we land." She lets out a shrill whistle and Fitz is by her side as she sweeps out of the bridge.

I'm really not sure if I'm proud of my feisty mate or as terrified as the rest of the warriors that stare after her.

"We're going to have to land in the Helix mountains." Bron has recovered himself sufficiently to be capable of speech.

"That's a long way from the Council. How are we going to get to Reelux?" It's at least a day of ground travel between the mountains and the capital of the north continent, where the Council resides.

"I've arranged air transport, but we've got to get to the valleys first," Bron massages his balls to the hidden amusement of Jak and Terx, "through the tunnels. Terx is from that region, he knows the way." He says in answer to my next question.

"In which case, I'll make sure my mate is properly prepared for such a trek."

43

JAYNE

I didn't fancy a meal on my own in the canteen, so I collected some of my favorites so far, including the *ovo* buns and some *juuli* fruit and took it back to our quarters. I'm longing for a cup of tea. It's a craving that, no matter what I do, I'm not going to be able to indulge. I've not even missed tea up until now either. Instead, I use the dispenser in the cabin to get a sort of savoury hot drink that the Haalux seem to like. It tastes like Bovril.

Fitz gets stuck into a couple of *ovo*, and several strips of what I was assured are a sort of meat. He and I are chomping happily when Rex enters.

"Hey." I offer him one of the buns.

He's still stinking of the alcohol from last night and could probably do with a mop up. I guess I shouldn't blame him, what with finding out his best buddy wasn't dead after all. Getting pissed together is a thing guys do, right? Once again, I'm reminded of just how little I know about relationships, at least relationships that involve me.

"Hey." He sinks down on the bed and takes the *ovo* gratefully. I also pass him the cup of hot liquid, which he practically inhales. "I didn't know you liked *Sool*."

"Is that what it's called? I just asked for a hot drink. Given that whatever you were drinking last night is off limits for me, that's all I can ask for." I pat my belly.

Rex looks anguished, and I know I'm being too hard on him. If I don't know what I'm doing, Rex certainly doesn't, and that essentially makes me a bitch.

"This whole mating thing is new for us both, Rex. I guess neither of us ever expected to be in this position." I heave myself onto his lap and snuggle against his hard chest as he wraps his arms around me.

"I thought I'd never find a mate. I was born from a forced mating, and we are taught that such children are considered unlikely to find their true mate. I expected to spend each of my Zycles on the machine. Now I know differently." Rex bends his head to kiss me and the touch of his heated skin rips through my body. "As much as I want to claim you, *kedves*," He murmurs hoarsely, his forehead on mine, "We'll be landing shortly, and I need to get you ready."

With that, he lifts me off his lap and deposits me on the bed, before striding across the cabin and opening a cupboard I had no idea was there. Talk about being left to stew in my own juices!

He rummages for a while, occasionally looking back at me, before he pulls out a number of garments and brings them over. There is a set of soft leather like pants, a fitted long-sleeved top, a long duster coat lined with some sort of buff colored fur and a set of soft mahogany colored boots.

"We have a way to travel before we reach Reelux, the main city on Haalux, my mate, and you need to be properly dressed. Not that I mind what you're wearing," His eyes heat as he looks me over. "I'd rather the rest of Haalux doesn't get as good a view."

"When you say you were born of a forced mating, what do you mean? I thought that if you were unable to mate you were sedated?" I ask as I pull on the clothing, which is a surprisingly good fit, even over my expanding middle.

"There have been some changes to the Haalux breeding programme since I was conceived," Rex explains. "At one time, despite the danger to females, the males were not restrained and simply introduced into a mating space with the female. The male would then rut her, regardless of her intentions. Later they invented the machine for the more violent males which took away any risks to the females in the process."

"The more you tell me about your society, Rex, the less I want to be part of it." I admit.

Rex laughs as he helps me on with the big coat. "Just how big is your world?" He asks.

"Earth? I don't know. It wasn't the biggest planet in our solar system, but the only one we believe can support life." I reply.

"And how many humans lived on it?"

"Probably around seven to eight billion, I think." I answer. Rex lets out a further bark of laughter.

"Such a tiny planet, sweet female. You have no idea, do you? The population of Haalux is around seventy billion, and that's just Haalux, not any other species that occasionally choose to make their home there. The planet is the largest in our system. If we are to have a population to come close to fulfilling our needs, then every effort has to be made to ensure continuance of our species."

Rex has moved close to me as he speaks, placing his hands either side of my small protruding pregnancy. He bends his head to kiss me on the lips, long and deep. "This little one is going to be a huge part of the Empire." He murmurs in my hair.

I'm not entirely sure what he means, and I'm still a bit annoyed that he has been so condescending to me about the size of Haalux and their strange practices. I don't care what he says, it's still sounds barbaric. Enclosed in his arms, I could almost forgive his species anything. Although when I find out who is responsible for fitting me up for a crime I didn't commit, there will be hell to pay.

"*Commander?*" The intercom on the wall fires up with the voice of one of the warriors I was introduced to yesterday, "*We're about to land, if you want to come to the bridge?*"

"Come and see my planet, *kedves*. Then you can make your own mind up about it." Rex nuzzles at my hair.

"When you put it like that, Rex, how can I refuse?"

I follow him through to the bridge, where there is a landing party assembled. From the viewing window I finally see Haalux. Rex's planet and my child's home. The warrior piloting the ship expertly maneuvers around the biggest snow-capped mountains I have ever seen. I thought the mountain ranges that I had encountered on Katahrr were big. I was wrong. You could fit them multiple times over inside one of the valleys we are flying down. They are huge, black and imposing, like something out of a fantasy novel. I hear a slight snigger to one side and spot Terx staring at me. I remember to close my mouth.

Occasionally I catch a glimpse of a large red orb, hanging low in the sky. "That's the Lux sun," Rex says in my ear from behind me. "It's a red giant some billions of miles away from Haalux. Our main sun is much closer."

"It's beautiful, Rex," There are no other words to describe it. I expected the planet to be big, but the awesome sight of the mountains and the red sun are overwhelming.

"I'm pleased you like it, my mate."

Seemingly out of nowhere, a landing platform appears, nestled in a side valley. The ship descends until it finally lands down with the slightest of bumps. I hadn't realized I was holding my breath until I feel us touch down.

"Let's go." Bron orders, and with Rex by my side, we are surrounded by warriors and head through the ship until we reach an airlock, now open to the outside.

A sharp wind, smelling of ice and metal, hits me in the face. I pull my coat closer around me and I'm pleased Rex made sure I was dressed for the occasion. As a group, we troop down a ramp towards a solitary Haalux warrior at the base.

"Torat?" Rex exclaims and steps forward to clasp the other Haalux by the forearm.

"And this must be the female causing all the trouble," The older Haalux reminds me of Jaal, except he lets his emotions show on his face. His red eyes twinkle at me. "Although it looks like trouble has found you." He places a hand on my rounded stomach, obvious even under my heavy coat. "Never one to stand still, eh, Rex?"

Rex places a comforting arm around my shoulder. "Forat and I go way back, although not as warriors. He was generally around to procure whatever he could by whatever methods he could. Fighting he would leave to others." He grins at Forat.

"Forat, you old rogue!" Bron strides up, "is everything ready?"

"Not standing on ceremony as usual, *Captain*," Forat grumbles. "Yes, everything's ready, what do you take me for, a Grolix?"

"I'm just going on past performance." Bron grins.

"It was one time!" Forat mutters. "And you still got what you needed."

I shiver in the biting wind that's blowing directly down the mountainside and all the males notice it. Not that I was trying to make a point or anything.

"This way," Forat heads off towards an opening that is more like a large crack in the side of the mountain. I hurry after him, keen to be out of the elements.

44

REX

Warm air blows from the entrance to the Helix cave system before we reach it. Even with the clothing I provided, Jayne was feeling the cold, and I'm glad when we reach the opening. From the look on her face, Jayne is too. Once we reach it, Fitz pops into existence and swarms onto Jayne's shoulders, much to Forat's interest.

"Is that a Masca?" He asks Jayne.

"This is Fitz." Jayne strokes the creature, and he chuckles to himself.

Forat reaches out a hand and I debate, briefly whether or not to warn him. It's an easy choice, one that wouldn't have troubled Forat for a minute. He manages to touch Fitz on his neck and, although the creature crackles, his form spiking slightly, he remains relatively calm.

"I thought them to be extinct, or at least very rare." He says, scratching Fitz behind his tiny ears.

"That's what I was told by the Katarrians. I tried to get him to return to the wild, but he seemed keen to stay with me." Jayne explains.

"They make very loyal pets, something that has been forgotten in the scramble for their pelts." Forat says with interest.

"We're ready to go," Terx calls out across from a set of five fully prepared hover-sleds. The first three are already loaded with the warriors that form part of Bron's ground party. The remaining two are for us. "We can follow the main route through to the first camp, where we'll rest overnight and then we should be able to reach the outer edge by nightfall."

"Fitz is not for sale." I say sternly to Forat, who is stroking his chin as he contemplates Fitz. He immediately adopts a hurt air, holding his hands up.

"Thought never crossed my mind." He says. I glower at him as I usher Jayne towards the sleds.

Once she's settled, with Fitz tucked into her coat and a comm link to me hooked over her ear, I mount up behind her. Terx gives the order and the party moves off into the caves. Initially they are lit with artificial lights, but this soon gives way to the bioluminescence from the plants growing within the system as we race deeper into the mountain.

"*What is this place?*" Jayne says over the link. Her eyes are wide and dark as she stares at the rushing walls.

"These mountains have been mined for an eternity by generations of Terx's ancestors. He is from an ancient tribe of Haalux known as the Arlix. They mined the mountains originally for precious metals and more recently for the fuel we require for space-flight." I explain. "The mining process encourages the *Niril*, the plant life you see on the walls."

Terx has started with an impressive pace we are able to keep up for a number of hours before he slows to allow us to rest. The warriors pile off their respective sleds and take up various positions around the tunnel. I'm impressed at their training, and it's good to see that some of what I drilled into Bron has rubbed off on him.

Jayne's fast asleep on the sled, and I decide not to wake her. There's nothing interesting about this part of our journey. Instead, I grab a bag of rations and sit on the ground. Almost immediately I feel a sleek, furry head pressing against my cheek. Fitz most certainly is awake, and he quickly noses his way to my bag. I give him a couple of slices of dried *Naxin* meat, which he chews on happily. The resting warriors have a similar idea, and the cave is quiet as they consume their food.

The silence makes the spectacular explosion that rips through the tunnel seem far louder than it actually is. The whole area immediately fills with smoke, dust and floating luminescent particles that are almost blinding. I'm on my feet to reassure Jayne, pulling my goggles over my eyes. She's covered in the dust and coughing.

"We need to get out of here," I call to her. Every instinct I have is making me protect my mate at all costs.

I know mining blasting when I hear it, and that wasn't such an explosion. As the ringing in my ears lessens, I can hear the sound of many footsteps heading our way. Our sled is undamaged, and I mount up.

"Hold on!" I yell out and gun the engine before firing us forward through the smoke as fast as the thing will go. A couple of figures loom at us through the settling dust and the sled glances off them. There's the sound of blaster fire behind us, and I return a couple of shots, but I don't look back. Bron can handle this one.

Eventually the smoke and dust thins as we race forward into the strange light of the caves. I need to get as much distance between us and whatever was going on back there before I try and contact Bron again.

"*Rex, can we stop, please?*" Jayne says, hoarsely over the comm link. I bring the sled to a halt and she rolls off, coughing hard.

I grab a canteen of water and pull her into my arms, helping her take a couple of sips until the fit subsides. Fitz appears by her side and nudges at her, his red eyes glittering with concern.

"What the hell was that?" Jayne finally manages to get out.

"I think it was aimed at us." There's no point hiding the truth from my mate; she'd find out soon enough.

"Where's everyone else?" She looks behind us into the glowing tunnel.

"There was some sort of fire fight. I needed to get you out of there. We'll catch up with them later."

"Thank you, Rex." Jayne's voice is almost inaudible, and for a second I'm concerned the dust might have injured her, then I see the water running from her eyes. "I know how hard it would have been for you to leave your warriors."

"Leaving my mate would have been harder, and Bron understands that." I give her a reassuring smile. Fact is, I didn't even think about them, getting her to safety was my first priority. The explosion wasn't designed to injure anyone, and Bron and his warriors are more than equipped to deal with whatever or whoever caused the blast. "We need to get off the main route until we can regroup with the others. Are you okay to walk for a bit?"

Jayne nods. She pours a little of the water into her hands and splashes it on her face. It's nice to see her pink skin again. I help her to her feet and put as much as I can into a pack, which I hoist onto my back.

"There's side tunnels all the way along the main tunnel. We should be able to pick one up pretty easily, but we're going to have to get rid of our ride."

I fire up the sled again and set it off down the tunnel. Hopefully if there's anyone following, they'll keep chasing the sled and it'll buy us some time.

"Ready?" I say to Jayne. She links her arm in mine and we start walking.

45

JAYNE

We've not been walking long down the main tunnel when Rex spots a hidden opening. I'm greatly relieved to be away from the larger tunnel. Every sound in there echoed and had me on edge. I've been abducted by aliens and drugged, twice. I've been abused and accused of a crime I didn't commit, but far and away that explosion was one of the scariest things that has happened to me, ever.

Fortunately, Rex has a cool, clear head and the way he navigated the sled thing through the mayhem was amazing. Seeing him like that, in full battle mode was an eye opener to say the least. I'm not going to lie; he was damn sexy and it thrilled me to my core.

Initially it's dark away from the main tunnel. Rex reaches around my chest and presses something onto my coat. It's a flat torch that gives out a strong beam of light, illuminating the way ahead. There's a set of roughly hewn steps in the shiny black rock that makes up the tunnels. I make my way carefully down with Rex at my back. Fitz scampers ahead of us. He was unfazed by the blast, other than getting rather spitty and angry at the dust. The narrow stairs open into a larger passage that is lit with the bioluminescent plants that also covered the walls of the main tunnel.

The plants are multi-colored, something it was impossible to see when we were on the sled rushing along. Their neon colours are some of the most beautiful I have ever seen. Some are fern-like, and others have small waving tentacles like sea anemones.

"What do they feed on?" I ask Rex in wonder as I touch one, its tentacles withdrawing into its body.

"I don't know much about this underground region; I believe they take their nutrients from the air." Rex replies.

As if to emphasize his statement, a strong, warm wind hits us. Presumably, there must be some sort of thermal vents in this cave system. As we walk further along the passage, the temperature starts to rise. I shrug off my coat and Rex does the same, his muscular chest bare, with only his weapon belt crossing it. His Hallan markings glow in the strange light. He takes my coat and stows it in his pack. He smiles down at me; although I can tell it's a little strained. I stand up on tiptoes to give him a reassuring kiss. If I didn't already believe he would keep me safe, I do now.

Rex cocks his head to one side. "Wait here." He says and starts to move away.

"No, I'm staying with you." I move in front of him. "There's no way you're leaving me here on my own."

Rex blinks at me, not entirely sure what to make of a stubborn female that doesn't take orders.

"Okay, stick close." He gently tucks me behind him.

"Oh yeah, because I'm going to go exploring on my own." I mutter as I follow him down the passage.

It starts to open into a larger gallery, filled with more greenery than bioluminescence and lit by artificial light.

"Looks like there's a camp." Rex says over his shoulder. We walk further into the cavern and it becomes clear that there are several smaller caves being used as dwellings. I see movement, and slowly, Haalux emerge. A much older male approaches us. His eyes are such a dark red, they are almost black, and he's stooped with age, his gray skin more iridescent than Rex's.

"I require somewhere for my mate to rest and access to your communications." Rex states.

The elderly Haalux lifts his head, carefully looking over Rex, and finally, he bows as low as his wizened frame will let him.

"Certainly, Sire." He says in a voice that is stronger and louder than his appearance would suggest. He shuffles off and starts motioning to other Haalux.

"Sire?" I look up at Rex, who is managing to hold a suitable regal bearing, without knowing he's doing it. I muffle a laugh, and he drops his gaze to me briefly before he returns to scanning his surroundings.

"Please?" I turn at the sound of a female voice. "If you will come with me?" The female Haalux is much taller than me, heavy set, but feminine face without Hallan. Her eyes are a piercing green color. She's dressed in tunic and trousers, her muscular arms bare as she motions me over to one of the smaller caves.

Rex nods at me, and I follow the female, Rex hot on my heels. The cave consists of a raised platform covered in furs, all very cave man, or cave-Haalux. I sit on the bed and Fitz swarms onto me, much to the surprise of the female.

"What is that creature?" She asks, her eyes glittering with interest.

"Fitz is a Masca from Katahrr," I explain. "You can stroke him if you want?" She reaches out a hand and touches Fitz on his back. He hums with pleasure and she smiles.

"I am Gelid." She says as she tickles Fitz under his chin.

"I'm Jayne and this is Rex."

"Commander Rexitor." Rex intones. I guess we're back to that.

"But he doesn't mind, Rex." I add with a grin, pleased to be bursting his bubble. He ignores me, staring out over the larger cave watchfully.

"Have you come from the outside?" Gelid asks. Rex lets out a low growl. "I'll get you some refreshments." She scurries out.

"That was fucking rude, Rex, they're only trying to be nice. You can drop the whole alpha male act." I spit over at him.

"There's something going on," He nods across the larger cave.

There is a group of Haalux, older males and more females gathered around the elder Haalux we first met in deep discussion. Whatever it is, it has Rex on edge. The group appear to have reached a decision and the elder Haalux advances across the cave towards us. Rex draws himself up to his full height.

"Sire," the elder Haalux addresses Rex again as he enters, "we are most honored by your presence. I am Barjin"

"Looks like they have heard of *Commander Rexitor* after all, Rex." I say sarcastically, interrupting the older male.

I'm tired and thirsty. It's even hotter in this cave than it was in the passage, and I'd just like to rest. My back is killing me too. I could definitely do without any more theatrics today. Barjin gives me an indulgent smile.

"We are honored with the presence of an *Istvon* and his mate." He says and appears to be going to attempt another bow.

"*Istvon*? I think not!" Rex snorts.

"What the hell is going on?" I ask, unable to read the elder's expression. Rex is simply glowering.

"*Istvon* is ancient Haalux for King, or more properly translated, great leader," Rex says to me, "I'm neither of these things. I'm a freak born from a forced mating. I'm no *Istvon*." He says, shaking his head angrily.

"On the contrary, *Istvon,* you bear the markings of a true king." Barjin traces his hand over the markings on Rex's chest. "And here is where your bloodline shows truly." He touches Rex's face, over his lower Hallan as Rex jerks his head away.

"No! You are mistaken." He roars, his patience with the older Haalux clearly at an end.

I'm on my feet and beside him, my hand on his arm.

"Look, Rex, maybe they are a bit backward here and have never seen a Haalux with your markings before. Don't be too hard on them." Rex huffs out a breath, his eyes hard.

"Maybe." He concedes. "Where is the communications I asked for?" He fires out at Barjin.

"I will bring it, *Istvon*." He smiles a gappy smile and hurries off again as fast as his gait will take him.

"I'm not *Istvon*!" Rex calls after him.

All that comes back in return is the sound of the old Haalux chuckling. Not that I blame him; it must be the Haalux version of an eye roll. I'm on the point of doing one myself at Rex's behavior. Being told you are a King is surely better than being chased away with pitchforks.

Gelid makes a welcome return, carrying a tray of food and a pitcher of clear liquid. Almost before she has placed it down on a low table, I'm pouring out a glass and downing it almost in one. It's cool, refreshing and slightly carbonated but not water.

"What is this?" I ask, pouring Rex a glass which he takes with poor grace.

"It's from the natural springs here. It passes through a number of different strata which results in its unusual flavour." Gelid says, knowledgeably. "I'm currently conducting some research into whether it has any properties that could assist in either the medical or scientific field."

"You're a scientist?" I query. "I thought that Haalux females were just breeders."

Rex shoots me a look that could, frankly, cut steel. Fortunately, Gelid laughs.

"Not quite," She pats her belly, which I notice is rounded like mine. "Our primary aim is to have happy, healthy Haalux children, but we gestate for twelve turns, and well, that's a lot of time on our hands. I'm part of the science corps in the Empire. I have a small team here working on the liquid from the natural springs. There's also a team of medics researching some of the minerals that seem to have healing properties in this region."

"You're pregnant?" I realize that's a really dumb question.

"With my tenth, would you believe?" Gelid grins at me and places her hand on my stomach. "Your first?"

I nod. Gelid lowers her voice. "His too?"

I nod again.

"Figures." She says quietly with a secret smile. "What species are you?" She asks.

"Human, you've probably not heard of them."

"Nope, that's a new species on me. Clearly compatible with

Haalux though." She winks. "And here's me thinking all our males were off world busy defending the Empire and seeking out new resources. Turns out they're mating whilst they're at it."

"Be careful what you say, female." Rex growls at her.

"Oh, shut up, Rex. She's joking." His bad mood is beginning to piss me off.

Gelid bows to Rex. "I meant no disrespect, *Istvon*."

"So you believe in this *Istvon* stuff too?" I sort of feel a bit better about it if Gelid does believe in it. She's a bit more grounded than the older Haalux who does seem away with the fairies.

"I don't have to believe in it. I did some research a few years ago that was repressed by the Council. Barjin was part of my team then as he is now." Gelid replies. "There is a genetically pure line of Haalux that predates the changes to the mating Zycle. They're only identifiable by the additional Hallan."

"There is research to prove my lineage?" Rex says, his voice quiet.

"I have it here with me," Gelid says. "And there is no way you were born from a forced mating, *Istvon*. Your parents must have been a mated pair. Now, eat and I'll see where Barjin has got with that communication device."

She leaves our cave with Rex staring after her.

"I have family?" He says after a moment's silence.

46

REX

Jayne puts her arms around my waist as I try and take in what the female, Gelid, has just told me.

The whole thing about being an *Istvon* seemed laughable. Initially I was inclined to Jayne's reasoning that we had stumbled on some sort of backwards tribe of Haalux that hadn't seen the light of day for some time. But Gelid has provided a rational explanation, and the merest hope that my rogue Hallan are not an accident of birth, but something more. Further, that I might have been born from love, rather than necessity.

My mate presses her lush body against mine. I can feel her rounded stomach, full of my child, and the beauty of being mated is revealed to me. I want her more than ever. I want to love her, protect her, and be with her. I want to make sure my daughter has the life I did not have, free from the ties that bind a Haalux to their mating Zycle. I want her to have a choice, to be like her mother if she wishes, or like her father.

I've spent my entire life trying to conform. That life was a lie.

"Penny for them?" Jayne kisses me on my jawline.

"I don't understand," I cuddle her closer, my funny little human.

"Just wondering what you're thinking." She says, her hand on my cheek and her dazzling blue eyes studying my face.

The elder Haalux bustles in, carrying an equally ancient communication device, meaning I don't have to answer Jayne's question. He hands me the device reverentially.

"It is all in working order, *Istvon*. Do you require any assistance?"

"No, Barjin, I can take it from here. I need to see Gelid, send her in." I tell him firmly.

"Why didn't you tell me about all of this?" Jayne asks, sitting down on the bed as I try to work the communicator.

"Tell you about what?" I say, distractedly. The tech is old but in working order, providing I can raise Bron on it, we should be able to meet up with him at the exit to the valleys, providing the science team can help us out.

"About your society, that females are your scientists and medics, not just baby machines." Jayne has an edge to her voice that makes me look up.

"I thought you meant the *Istvon* thing?"

"What? That you're some sort of Haalux royalty because you look different to the others? I didn't need a DNA test to tell me you were special, honey." She replies. "Where I come from, loads of people have links to royalty through their family line. I don't know why you didn't tell me what your females actually do."

"I think the question is why you thought that way. Probably says more about your primitive society values than that of the Haalux." I reply without thinking.

The communicator crackles into life and I input the code for Bron. Although I was confident he could handle what went on back with some considerable relief that I get an answering code and connect to Bron.

"*Brother!*" He fires out, "*Are you and your mate safe?*"

"We are, Bron. How's your team?"

"*Safe. Once our assailants found you missing, resistance was limited. I'm pleased they didn't find you.*"

"What happened back there?" I ask.

"*We were betrayed, Rex. I'm sorry. It was Terx.*" I can hear the anger in Bron's voice over the communicator.

"Did you deal with him?"

"*The fucking traitor got away, but he will pay for what he's done.*" If I know Bron, that's a threat he will definitely carry out. "*We need to meet up.*"

"I'm going to find out how far we are from the valley entrance then I'll contact you with an ETA, brother."

"*Recon in ten.*" Bron terminates the communicator at his end. Hopefully, our conversation was short enough to stop anyone pinpointing our locations.

"We need to find out where we are, then we can arrange to meet up with Bron." I say to Jayne.

Or at least I would have, if she was still there. Our cave is empty, save for Fitz, who is happily curled up in the center of the bed. He opens one red eye, stares at me and closes it again with a big sigh. My mind goes back to our earlier conversation and my stomach sinks. I insulted her species, and I didn't answer her question.

I stride out into the central cave. Gelid is stood to one side, speaking with a number of other female Haalux, at least two of which are as pregnant as her. She looks over as I approach and bows, which is starting to grate on my already appalling mood. I hate being apart from Jayne.

"*Istvon*, can I assist?"

"You can stop calling me *Istvon*, Commander will do. I need to know where my mate is, and how far we are from the valley entrance." I snap at her. I also want more of an explanation from her, but that can wait.

"It's ten clicks to the valley entrance. As for your mate, Barjin took her to see the thermal waters," Gelid notices the dark look on my face. "She asked to go." She taps her fingers on her expanding stomach and gives me a searching look. "There's more to being a mated male than just sex and testosterone, Commander."

"I know, or rather I don't know," I lower my head and pinch the bridge of my nose, clearly this female knows that I've upset my mate. "I never expected to be a mated male. All I know is how to fight."

"And lead, from what I hear." Gelid says, "I looked you up, we're not so far underground that we don't have access to the central net." I raise my eyebrows at her, "Don't worry. I'm not stupid. It's clear you're not here on a social visit. I used an incognito protocol. there will be no trace of my search."

"We need to talk about all of this *Istvon* stuff, but after I have found my mate, and apologized."

"At least you have your priorities right," Gelid smiles at me. "Follow that passage over there, it'll take you to the springs. When you've made up with your mate, we'll talk. You'll need to stay here for the night and continue on to the valley in the morning."

I return to the smaller cave and communicate the plan to Bron. Then I quickly head down the passageway indicated by Gelid to find Jayne. After several turns the passageway opens out into a series of small caverns. I can hear the sound of splashing up ahead of me, which makes me increase my pace. I reach a cave that is lit only by the bioluminescence of the plants that throng the tunnels, only far more than I've seen so far. There's a large pool that appears to be glowing, in the center of which is my mate.

Naked.

She spots me and turns away, floating down the pool with ease.

"Wait, Jayne!" I call after her, my voice echoing in the chamber.

I pull off my boots and step up to the edge of the pool, hesitating. I pull off my trousers too and take a step, gingerly, into the liquid. It's warm and tingling on my skin. Jayne is still ignoring me and heading further away. Initially there is a set of shallow shelves, then the floor drops away sharply. I push off, hoping I'll float.

I don't. I sink instead.

47

JAYNE

I can't even put into words just how angry I am with Rex. So angry tears are running down my face as I leave the small cave and rush into the main one. My vision blurred as I come up against a soft gray mound of flesh.

"Hey," Gelid says, holding me to her. "Everything okay."

"Yeah, just feeling a bit claustrophobic in there." I stifle a sniff.

"Sure you are, sweetness." Gelid gives me a squeeze. "Haalux males are an acquired taste."

"I care for Rex. I really do." I smooth my hand over my rounded belly. "But we've not had much time to get to know each other and he can be a bit—" I search for the expression, "full on alpha male sometimes."

"Not something your species is used to?"

"Oh god, yes! Human society is full of males that think they're alpha. I'm used to dealing with 'little man' syndrome." I think of all the times I've been up against a senior partner or barrister in court who thinks that a woman is a pushover. Their decision to rely on gender stereotypes was their downfall. As a lawyer I was every bit as vicious and ruthless as my male counterparts, worse even. "I'm just not used to the concept of fated mates. That's taking some headspace."

Gelid laughs, "I guess we're lucky females. We get all the advantages of being mated without having to deal with the males."

"So, basically, Haalux is run by females?"

"Not exactly," Gelid's face tightens. "There is a single female on the Council of Three and Assembly are all males. It is to the advantage of Haalux society that females pursue whatever profession they wish, as long as they breed. So we do, for the good of the Empire."

It sounds ultimately as silly as most human societies. I guess I expected more from a species that is so obviously light years ahead of the Human race. Although equally, they've probably had more time to cock it all up.

"How about you have a relax in the thermal springs?" Gelid ventures with a smile.

The water is a delicious temperature, and as soon as Berjin has left, I've stripped off my clothes and I'm straight in. My expanding body is buoyant and it's like swimming in a wetsuit. I'm floating happily when I hear Rex call out. I'm not ready to speak to him yet, and I swim further away, childish I know. It's not like the guy has crossed the Galaxy to find me or anything. He can damn well swim to me, too.

There's a splashing sound behind me and I swirl in the water to see Rex's head disappearing under. I assume he's just messing about until he reappears, splashing and gasping. In a flash I've swum over to him.

"Don't panic! I've got you." I swim just out of his reach, grabbing under his chin. I tow him back to the shallow shelves at the edge of the pool, where he lies spluttering, his head in my lap.

"What happened?" I ask, gently stroking his brow to calm him, his orange eyes are almost starting out of his head.

"I don't know how to float in the water like you." He coughs. It's suspiciously pathetic.

"You don't know how to swim? Why did you get in the water then?" Stupid mate.

"I wanted to be with you." Rex says, his voice small. I think my suspicious are correct, but the woeful expression that Rex is managing to keep on his face is melting my heart.

Damn, it's hard to stay mad at him.

"I'd better give you some mouth to mouth, just to be sure you're okay." I bend my head and press a kiss to his lips.

Rex responds strongly, his hands reaching for my breasts, running his thumbs over my hardening nipples. I reach for him. He's already rock hard, his cock ramrod straight against his abs. He deserves to be tortured for giving me such a fright, but as my core pulses and his eyes glow with lust, instead I pull him to a lower shelf, so that I can use the water to give me buoyancy and grace.

Initially he struggles then he realizes what I'm doing, and his hands find my waist, guiding me so that I'm astride him. I rub myself against his thick shaft. Actually, I am going to tease him a little.

'Are you sure you're up to this? After all you nearly drowned." I lean over him, my stomach and breasts pressed on his chest as I kiss up his jaw to his ear as I move my crotch up and down over his cock, feeling his hips buck as he tries to get inside me. "I couldn't possibly request sex from my male if he's not up to full strength."

"My sweet and delectable mate, I'd do anything for you." Rex groans.

"Anything to be buried up to your balls in my pussy, you mean." I push off from the shelf and swim away from him, just out of his reach in the deeper part of the pool. "That's what got us into this trouble in the first place." I float on my back, showing my rounded belly to a muted roar from him.

"Please, my gorgeous mate, come back. I promise to tell you everything and I'll do anything you ask." Rex is stroking himself in the shallows, a look of pain on his face.

I bob in the water, allowing my breasts to break the surface and Rex's eyes widen. Then, with a few short kicks, I'm back over him. He grabs at me, hunger in his eyes and flips me over, pushing me further into the shallows, he presses his cock at my entrance, soaking with my juices and he enters me with one hard thrust, moaning in delight as my pussy walls embrace him fully. He grasps my butt cheeks, his fingers digging into my flesh. He thinks he's in control, but as he withdraws to thrust again, I push back on him, letting him go deeper than ever and he moans in response, his hand reaching around to touch my clit. He gently caresses the tender nub as he increases his strokes, and I move with him, using the shallow water to my advantage. Rex is an excellent lover and a quick learner, heeding the call of my body along with his.

He's needy now, his thrusts increasing in fervor, wanting to fuck away all his worries, about who he is and what the future holds. I'm more than willing, not only to help him, to enjoy his hard, thick length, pounding me, but because I know I've embraced my life as it is. Far from home, pregnant and hunted. I've got a mate who wants me, loves me even, in his own way.

"My mate," Rex croons as his finger explores my clit and soft folds, feeling himself thrusting into me. "My *kedves*,"

The heat from his Hallan on his cock is intense, the tingling the strongest I've ever felt before, almost like a vibration. When it hits, my orgasm is shattering. Rex grips at my hips as I come apart, shuddering, my walls clasping and pulsing over his shaft, I see stars in my vision as it fades, every inch of my being exploding in the pleasure my mate brings me. Dimly I feel his own convulsions as he releases himself into me, groaning his climax as he collapses into the warm water, pulling me over his muscular body, arms wrapped tight around my changing form.

Holding me as if he will never let go.

48

REX

My sweet, pregnant female snuggles in my arms and I cover her with some furs. I suspect I may have exhausted her with our recent activities. I certainly hope that the science team are not using that pool for the liquid they drink.

I'm finally relaxed. The last half a day was full on, not least being told that I'm of a genetically pure Haalux line with the future of the Haalux race in my mate's belly. Or that's what Gelid implied when we returned from our time in the pool.

"You said the Council repressed your research, why?" I look through the data device she has given me. Most of it beyond my comprehension other than a few elements relating to the genetic lineage and Hallan markings.

"I'm not entirely sure. They definitely didn't want it in general circulation. I was made to give up all copies and sent here with my entire team. Sure, the research we are doing here is important but-"

"Keeping you here is the best way to bury bad news?" Jayne pipes up.

Her hair is wet, slicked back over her head and her skin is glowing. It looks like the liquid we have been bathing in has done her the world of good. She sits next to Gelid, one hand resting on her stomach.

"We have limited contact with the rest of Haalux and our research grant is for a full five turns, so sending us here was calculated." Gelid nods. "I guess the Council thinks the population isn't ready for what I found."

"Yet you kept a copy," I stare at her. Haalux females can be calculating when they want to be, or so I've been told.

"Insurance," Gelid holds my gaze. "I don't want some other Haalux taking credit for my research."

"Makes sense. I'd do that too." Jayne says as she takes the data device from me and starts to flick through it, studying it carefully. "What exactly does it mean for Rex though?"

A number of emotions flicker over Gelid's face before she speaks. "You know I said I had never met a human before?"

Jayne cocks her head to one side, looking at her intently.

"For a primitive species, you catch on quickly." She smiles at Jayne. "That is exactly the right question."

"So?"

"It means that Rex is from a pure genetic line, since before our scientists messed with things to try and ensure a greater birth rate and stronger warriors. It means that he originates from the lines that originally ruled Haalux and were bred out to give the Council more power and to take it away from those who knew how to use it wisely."

"But the genetic modifications were meant to improve Haalux. They have improved Haalux." I say, still unsure how I fit with all this.

"Surely you have felt the call of leadership. You were a leader until the Council deemed you not to be, and you were a good one. You've been repressed as much as my research has." Gelid says. "You and your offspring are the future of Haalux, where we move into a new age." Her eyes twinkle.

"A new age of what?"

"The other thing the Council has been repressing is that the genetic changes are no longer working. Despite appearances," Gelid strokes her own rounded stomach, "birth rate is falling again, dramatically. Did you know that there have been no conceptions in the last turn? My child was one of the final matings before the rate dropped off a cliff."

Jayne looks at me, shocked. "Jaal says we probably conceived the first time we-" She shoots a look at Gelid, her pink skin deepening in colour delightfully. "-had sex." It comes out as almost a whisper.

"That's just the point. We need proper matings, not just any mating. We need to increase our gene pool by embracing other compatible species and the Council doesn't want any of this, despite the fact that in any mating the Haalux genes remain dominant."

"I still don't see where I come into all this?" I say, trying to digest the implications for my species.

"The only way to move forward is to have an *Istvon* in charge. That is ultimately the reason my research was hidden by the Council. They don't want to admit to what is happening because it means a change in leadership and a change in our culture." Gelid says, her expression serious. "I just never expected that we'd find an *Istvon*. So many of them were culled."

There is a gasp from Jayne. "Culled?" She turns to me and I hold up my hands.

"I'm not defending that, not at all. There is nothing in our society that would ever make that acceptable." I try and reassure her as she shrinks away from both me and Gelid.

"I only found out about it when it became clear what the Council was going to do. I did my own digging and there were records that showed the Council sought out any Haalux that displayed evidence of additional Hallan and had them quietly disappeared." Gelid says, quietly.

"Please tell me you kept those records." I ask. Gelid smiles and nods.

"Haalux needs you, *Istvon* Rexitor. It needs, you, your mate, and your children. Without you, Haalux will crumble and die."

Gelid's words run around my head, meaning that, even with my mate slumbering in my arms, I can't sleep. How is it possible that I go from being an outcast, having to prove myself every step of my life to being something rare and wanted? Jayne shifts in my arms, murmuring something. Her eyelids flutter as she twitches in her sleep, her brow furrowed. She lets out a little cry and I bend my head to quiet her, kissing her gently on the forehead. She relaxes again, pressing her lush stomach into me. She's been through so much and yet she stands at my side. Jaal had been correct all that time ago when he described her as strong. She'll have to be to face what will come next.

49

JAYNE

My activities with Rex were the final straw. My poor pregnant body was begging for sleep by the time we had finished going over everything Gelid had. My mind was a different matter, whirling with everything she had said about Rex, about Haalux and about the Council.

Not that it was enough to keep me from sleep, even if my dreams were difficult, full of explosions and cages. I awake to a fully clothed Rex kissing his way over my naked body. Horny male.

"Good morning, my mate, did you sleep well?" He grins at me.

"You know I did." I love seeing him smile.

He kisses his way up my breasts, lingering on my sensitive nipples, enough to make me squirm, before he moves up to my lips. His Hallan heat as I enjoy a long, slow snog until I release a panting Rex, his eyes clouded with desire. He's still got a lot to learn, and I want to be the one to teach him.

'What's the plan for today?"

"We've got to meet up with Bron and the others," Rex pouts a little as he realizes he's probably not going get any this morning.

"They're okay?" I cry out. "Why didn't you say?"

Rex captures a nipple in his mouth and laps at it. "We sort of got caught up in other things." He mumbles.

I laugh and push him away as Fitz pops into existence next to me.

"How long has he been there?" Rex cries out.

"It's Fitz. Who knows." I give Rex a naughty smile, pulling on my clothing as Rex frowns at the Masca who chitters back at him.

"I got in contact with Bron yesterday. He and his team are fine. We were betrayed by Terx."

"Terx? The guy who knew these caves? So, basically this was a trap." Just when I thought things couldn't get any worse.

"It looks as if it was planned that way, even if it didn't work out for our assailants. Although I think with the information we have obtained from Gelid, our detour was informative." Rex replies, looking thoughtful.

"How are we going to protect Gelid? If you reveal yourself to the Council, what's to say they won't try and permanently repress her findings, along with you, me and her team?"

What we were walking into before we found all of this out was a million to one chance. I feel that our odds just got longer. There's so much at stake it almost makes my head want to explode.

"Gelid knows how to take care of herself, *kedves*. She's survived this long because she understands the politics. As for our future, you know I'll protect you, regardless." Rex has me in his arms and is burying his head in my hair, one hand on my stomach. "You mean everything to me. I'm never going to let you go." He holds me tight, and for a brief instant, I know what it is to be part of a mated pair.

"Gelid is going to let us have a hover-sled and give us directions to the valley from here. We'd better get going." Rex says as he puts me down.

I give Fitz a low whistle, and he's draped around my neck, buzzing with excitement as I follow Rex out into the main cavern. I'm guessing he's already seen the sleds and it's some comfort that he's not put off traveling on them after the last time. I wish I felt the same. Once we're out of these caves, I'm back in a world that wants me dead for something I didn't do.

Rex strides about, ordering the Haalux scientists and medics that form part of Gelid's team to attend to various tasks. He does it with grace and good humor. I can see in him what his friend Bron saw. He's a natural leader, even if he doesn't want to admit it to himself because he thinks he made a mistake. I'm too busy watching his tight muscular arse in those leather pants to notice Gelid, so when she puts her hand on my arm, I jump.

"He's a good looking male," She says, following my gaze. "I think every Haalux male should have a female that looks at them the way you do." She smooths her hand over her stomach. "That's what I want for this one anyway. No good comes from a society where more than half the population never experiences a loving touch." She has a faraway look in her brilliant green eyes.

"No society is perfect, but there's nothing wrong in striving for what is right." I reply.

"You're not just a sweet, primitive pet, are you?" Gelid grins at me, and I know she's joking. "You've both got a task in front of you, and I don't envy you at all. But from what I hear, you're more than up to it."

"I don't think I have much choice, Gelid," I hold my belly. "I've always fought for others, and now it's time to think of my own."

Rex turns and motions at me. I feel Gelid press something in my hand. It's a necklace, the chain so fine I can hardly see it. A series of gold bars hang from it. "For the future." She says and pushes me in the direction of Rex.

"Are you ready?" He asks as I settle myself on the body of the sled, whilst he is stood behind me at the controls. "I'm going to have to push it to meet up with Bron."

I pull the necklace over my head and tuck it inside my clothing. Gelid waves across at us.

"Punch it!" I shout at Rex. I've always wanted to say that.

"Punch what?" He asks and I twist to look into his confused face. The moment has gone.

"Let's go, Rex." I sigh.

There is a whine as the engines on the sled fire up and it lifts off the ground, swaying a little. Without much warning, it shoots forward and I'm pinned into the furs with the force of the movement. We shoot out of the cavern and down a narrow tunnel. The flora adorning the walls becoming a neon blur as we pass through at speed.

50

REX

We stop once in our journey through the cave system for something Jayne called a 'comfort break'. It meant her scurrying off to find a side passage whilst I held onto Fitz to prevent the Masca from following her.

"We're coming up on the exit," I tell her over the comm after we have been traveling for a few more hours. The mapping system on the sled fired into life a short while ago, indicating we were close enough to the outside world to start receiving a signal.

"*Thank god for that!*" She replies. "*Have you heard from Bron?*"

"I got a message earlier. They are waiting for us with transport to Reelux."

"*I hope it's more comfortable than this thing.*" I hear her mutter, and the sled wobbles as she shifts her weight.

Finally, we see natural light up ahead and Jayne leans forward to get her first real glimpse of Haalux. I keep the sled at a steady pace, just in case there are any issues, but I'm pleased Bron and his team, along with probably the oldest planet transport I've ever seen, wait for us at the cave entrance. We come to a halt, and Bron is immediately by Jayne's side, helping her to her feet.

"Rex!" He embraces my forearm, and I draw my Jayne away from him and to my side. She's too busy grumbling and rubbing at her bottom to notice.

"What happened back there?" I check around at his warriors. A few are sporting minor injuries. The only one missing was Terx.

"Usual rough and tumble. More to the point. What happened to you and your mate?" Bron casts a quizzical look at Jayne who is now dancing from foot to foot.

"We met an interesting group of scientists, one of which had some disturbing news." I explain. "Nothing that's going to make our next steps any easier." I raise an eyebrow at the transport. "Could you not have found a relic from the past we could use? I feel that this is too modern for me."

"Needs must, Rex. You're going to have to slum it for a while. You've gone soft traveling on the *Excelsior*." Bron holds out his hand to Jayne. "If my lady would care to join us?"

Jayne looks up at the transport. "Does this thing fly?" She says to Bron, incredulously.

Even she's concerned. The thing is a battered tube of silver ion metal, one large loading door and four engines mounted on each of the landing pillars. Black soot coats the sides of the craft where the engines are positioned in flight. It's hardly confidence inspiring, or a good introduction to a world and a species that are far advanced compared to hers.

"Everyone's a critic," Bron sighs. "Even the primitive species." His insult earns him a punch on the arm from Jayne and a visit from a spiky ball of crackling black fur that dances in front of him, whilst I laugh.

Bron signals to his warriors, and we load up on the transport.

"Seriously, Rex," Jayne hisses at me as we walk up the main ramp, and I show her through to the seating area, which is not much better than the exterior, several banks of bench seats, arranged in a number of squares, the upholstery is stained and ripped in places. "Is this thing really safe?"

"Sure." I give her the most reassuring smile I can. "I need to speak to Bron about Gelid and her research. Will you be okay here?"

Jayne makes a sour face at the seating but sits anyway, looking like she'd rather not touch it. I spot Jak, Bron's second in command.

"Jak? Where is your Captain?" I call over. He approaches, looking at Jayne as if she might explode.

"He's talking to the pilot about the best route to the city." Jak replies.

"Please look after my mate for me, see she gets what she needs." I say and move away quickly before the young warrior has a chance to protest.

Bron and Forat are speaking with the pilot on the small bridge of the transporter. Bron claps the warrior on his shoulder, and he starts the lift off process, the engines of the craft roaring with the effort of gaining height.

"We're going to go for a landing as close to the Council chamber as we can manage. This old thing hasn't got much in the way of tracking tech so, that might make things easier." Forat says, staring out of the window as the craft moves forward and out across the valley floor.

"Providing no one thinks to look up," Bron adds.

"The closer we are. The less resistance we should encounter." Forat says, ignoring Bron's comment. "They know we are coming. Providing we can be unorthodox in our approach, we should make it in with minimum casualties."

"Terx?" I raise my eyebrows at Bron.

"I thought his loyalty lay with me, but it appears he has been influenced. We have had word that his tribe has disappeared. Either it is because they are at war with the Empire or-"

"The Unseen?" I interrupt.

"I'd like to think he didn't betray me lightly." Bron says, his face clouded with anger. "I'd have preferred to have got hold of him, rather than him being out there, potentially revealing our plans."

"On our little detour, I found out a number of things that may or may not be related to our new enemy." I pull out my data device. I had Gelid download her research onto it before we left. "It appears that we are experiencing the worst drop in our birthrate since the modifications to our DNA a century ago." I shove the pad at Forat, who scrolls through it, frowning. "And the information is being kept from the populous."

"Do you think the infiltration of The Unseen is related?" Bron asks as he peers over Forat's shoulder.

"A new enemy and a strike at the very heart of the Empire, our ability to renew our population? It has to be related!" I reply. "Further, Hardag told Jayne that his allies wanted her as a breeder. I believe he meant The Unseen, and that they have other plans for our species."

"Says here that Haalux with Hallan like yours are *Istvon*." Bron is looking at the data-pad over Forat's shoulder. He breaks out into laughter. "There haven't been *Istvon* for centuries!"

Forat says nothing. He remains staring at the pad until he raises his eyes very slowly to meet mine. There is a pain and a recognition there.

"You knew?" My voice comes out as a hoarse whisper. "You knew and you said nothing?"

I've known Forat all my life. He's always been there, when I was in the breeding pool, when I was at the academy. Forat was always around to help me out, to give words of encouragement.

"I was assigned to you from the day your parents gave you up, for your own safety." Forat says, his voice low and gruff. "It's true. Rex is *Istvon*." He says to Bron. "He is our leader. His parents were a mated pair, the direct descendent of *Istvon* Hax and his true mate, Tiyan. The Council at the time of Rex's birth, wanted him out of the way because they saw him as a direct threat to their authority. Later Councils have sought to bury the concept of *Istvon* and promote their own version of what is right for Haalux."

"A version that has destroyed us." Bron has the pad and is swiping through the information given to me by Gelid, his eyes widening in horror.

"Not if it can be changed. Not if we can stop the Zycle mating and allow new genes into our species. As Forat and I have done."

"This is what they are promoting, The Unseen. They're using our system against us. If the current Council remains in power, we die out, and they get the Empire." Bron says, his tone hushed.

"I'm not going to Reelux to ask for a fair trial, Bron. We've got to gain control, to ensure the Empire knows of this betrayal, of The Unseen." I place a hand on his shoulder. "It's treason, and if we fail, we'll all be executed. I won't order you to do anything, but I would be honored if you would fight by my side."

"Like you even have to ask." Bron grins at me.

51

JAYNE

The transport thing rises off the ground, shaking like an old 737 airplane. It seems every nut and bolt, or whatever is holding this rust bucket together, is trying to work loose.

"Fuck!" I exclaim. The Haalux warrior, Jak, looks terrified at my outburst.

"Are you okay, mistress?" He asks.

"Please tell me this is normal?"

Jak looks around him. The rest of the Haalux warriors are sitting, chatting, eating, or relaxing. I suspect he's wondering why he's been assigned female watching duty.

"It's normal?" He replies and attempts a smile.

"We're all going to die," I mutter to myself and turn to look out of the window next to me.

What I see takes my breath away. The black mountains we landed in gave me no idea what sort of planet I was coming to. We rise over a lush orange and red forest, beyond which are acres upon acres of stunning bright green grasslands, dotted with clumps of the forest. The transport gathers speed and the rattling stops as we swoop over the terrain far more gracefully than I thought was possible.

"Hey." Rex sits down next to me, one arm around my waist. "What do you think?"

"It's stunning, Rex. Like nothing I've ever seen before." I breathe.

"I look forward to showing more of Haalux to you," Rex snuggles his face in my hair and kisses me. "For now we are heading to Reelux, where we intend dealing with the Council."

"What do you mean by 'dealing', that sounds ominous." I reply, curling my hand around his neck to ruffle his feather hair.

"We're going to give them a choice, to come clean or to abdicate and allow the assembly to appoint someone else in their place. The assembly is made up of Haalux from throughout the Empire representing various cities, tribes and land masses."

"But if that's done at the end of a blaster, isn't that a coup?" I pull back from Rex to be able to see his face.

"We won't use force, other than to gain an audience, if we need to." Rex says. I can't quite fathom what he means and I'm not entirely sure I want to think about it.

"How long before we get there?" I ask, averting my eyes from his to look out of the window.

What I see answers my question. It's a city like no other, looming on the horizon. The buildings spiral into the air, multiple rings piled on top of each other, spikes running from each one, like tendrils reaching out. It is a city in the clouds. A city of steel and glass. A city that would kill a creature for a crime she didn't commit. The sight of Reelux brings it home to me exactly where I am, a long, long way from Earth, facing down a powerful alien nation with nothing more than words and the child growing in my belly.

"Oh," I make a sound that is more of a swallow than a word. "That's not intimidating at all."

Rex curls his hand around mine, drawing my attention back to him.

"It is what it is. I am not intimidated." His voice is low and purposeful.

Nothing intimidates this male, not finding out his birth was a lie or the task ahead of us. He has become the center of my world. He grounds me in a way nothing has ever done before, not my love of the law or any previous relationships. He is full on and unstoppable.

The engine noise reaches a higher pitch, and it sounds like the pilot has changed gear.

"We're going to try and get as close to the Council as possible. Apparently, that was the plan with this old transport, it has little tech to track it. We are hoping to have reduced resistance when we land." He explains. "Which will be in a few minutes."

"As long as no one looks up anyway," I say, and Rex grins at me.

We're flying over the outskirts of the city now. Red coloured trees interspersed by low buildings that could be dwellings give way to taller, square ones that are more metal than glass. The warriors in the cabin are quiet, sitting in rank rows, they contemplate each other. I notice Rex has strapped on a long sword of some kind as well as the ubiquitous weapons bandolier across his chest that holds his blaster.

"Any chance of a weapon to defend myself?" I ask, suddenly feeling rather exposed. Rex looks affronted. "I know you'll defend me, but I don't want to be completely helpless."

He frowns. "I don't want you to be a target, which you will be if you're armed." I see him weighing up his decision, then he reaches around his back and brings out a small dagger in a sheath. "Make sure it's well concealed and don't show it unless you have to. The warriors we will encounter will not hesitate to kill you, regardless of whether you are a female or with child."

His words send a chill through me. If I wasn't already aware of just how much is at stake, that's made it clear. I shiver involuntarily, and Rex pulls me into him as the transport lurches downwards. There's the sound of laser fire glancing off the fuselage. Bron appears in the doorway to his cabin and motions to his warriors who swiftly exit. Bron sports the same sword as Rex along with double bandoliers over his chest. He looks every inch a pirate captain.

"You ready, Rex?" He asks.

"It would appear that I was born ready." Rex says grimly.

He helps me to my feet, and I tuck the dagger into the top of my right boot. Rex nods in appreciation of my chosen hiding place. With a comforting hand in the small of my back, he steers me through the transport until we reach the loading area. The ramp is already lowered, even though we are still hundreds of feet in the air. A hot wind whips through the opening, blowing me back into the hard, muscular form of my mate. A number of Bron's warriors are crouched at the door, large rifle like blasters in hand. Occasionally one of them lets off a laser round in a precise manner. We are descending rapidly, and I stumble as the craft lurches to one side, spinning around as we hit the ground. Rex turns me to face him.

"Whatever happens, you have to trust me," Rex says, fiercely, pressing his forehead against mine. "I love you, my mate, my *kedves*. You are mine entirely and forever."

"And I love you, Rex." The words tumble out of me unbidden. And I know it's my true feelings even before I've said the words. I've never wanted anyone like I want him. I have no idea how far I am from Earth, and I don't care anymore. Being with Rex, a male who believes in me like he does, who came for me like he did, has made me realize that it's the person you are with that is important, and that in turn is the life you live. It's real, tangible, and everything.

"Forever," I whisper as I press my lips against his, and we follow Bron's warriors into the light.

52

REX

The blaster fire starts as soon as we exit the transport. I push Jayne behind me and return fire at the handful of warriors stationed around the Council building. There's fewer than I expected, but then who in their right mind would attack the seat of the Haalux Empire?

Bron's warriors do a good job of picking off those with the better aim, dropping them with either stun shots or well-placed blaster bolts to put them out of action for a while. It's not long before the return fire ceases, and the dust begins to settle.

We've put down in the gardens to the front of the chamber, which is looking worse for wear following our battle. I never liked the formality of it anyway.

"*We've got the door!*" Bron shouts over my communicator. There's a dull whump as he detonates the hax explosives.

I take Jayne by the hand, and keeping an eye out, we make our way swiftly from the gardens through to the main door of the building, a huge edifice, built in the traditional style with additional spires that are designed to look like Hallan markings.

"I brought the key," I grin at Bron when I see the mess he's made of the door. "I guess you didn't need it?'

"Made my own." He replies and checks his wrist. "The main Council Guard are still ten minutes away. That should give us enough time to reach the chamber and lock it down."

"Why's the Guard not at the Council?" I query as we crunch our way over the debris of the door and into the building.

"I think that someone might have sent them on an errand." Bron nods across at Forat who gives me a thumbs up, the wily old Haalux.

Bron's warriors fan out through the main atrium and start to fire climbing pins upwards. They hit their marks and a number of them quickly attach themselves, shooting upwards to ensure there is a clear path.

"Looks like we made enough noise to clear the place anyway," I remark on the emptiness of the building, until I see a group of Haalux assembly members cowering behind a large planter. I fire a bolt over their heads just to be sure of their compliance.

"Are you going to be able to use the climber?" I ask Jayne as I run a strap around her distended abdomen. I remember her on the Grolix ship, so at least she has no problem with heights.

"How does it work?"

"Put your hand through here and hold this button down. Use your hand pressure to increase or decrease your ascent rate." I put her hand through the driver loop and show her how to stand on the foot loop.

"See you at the top." She laughs at me and fires herself upwards.

"Looks like your mate was made for combat," Bron says in my ear. "Lucky Haalux." He's on a climber now and is dragged upwards away from me before I can reply. I quickly strap myself on and in seconds I've reached the upper levels where there is a small group waiting for me.

"Status?" I look across at Bron.

"Five minutes for the Guard. We need to secure the Council of Three and the chamber before they get here as its going to be a shit-show once they do." He flicks his hand and three of his warriors, including Jak peel off from the main group and head into the spire that contains the council chamber. There's a couple of muffled explosions, and Bron holds his ear.

"It's secure. Let's go." He sets off at a steady jog, and we follow until we reach an area that is full of slowly dissipating smoke. "Good job," Bron calls out. The door to the chamber is open, but intact, and we are able to walk in.

Jayne stares around at the place. The last time she was here was in digital form, fighting for her life. Yet she doesn't look frightened. She's simply taking it all in, analyzing and comparing the one with the other. There's a loud groan as two of Bron's warriors push the doors closed and set about sealing them shut.

"The Council of Three, where are they?" I call across to Bron.

"We are here, Commander Rexitor." A booming voice rings through the chamber, so loud that Jayne covers her ears. "Explain your intrusion."

I look up and on the raised balcony, three hooded figures stand, waiting.

"Come down and face me, then I'll explain." I call out. Never allow your enemy to have the high ground. "Providing you are not going to hide behind your voice enhancer and forcefield. Presumably you are Haalux enough to speak to me face to face." It's a calculated risk, but there's no way we can get at the three if they remain on the balcony. Any Haalux should respond to being called a coward.

The three turn to each other, and it appears a decision is made. For an instant they disappear, then a hidden door slides open at the bottom of the balcony and the three step out to face us.

"We see you have brought your mate, Commander. Another aberration to the Haalux Empire." The voice from earlier comes from the central figure. I step forward, my hand on my psi-damascus sword. Bron steps in front of me, using his arm to hold me back.

"And Captain Bron, fresh from the slave planet," This voice comes from the council member on the left. It is sneering and it's my turn to grab hold of Bron.

He might be putting on a front for his men, but I've known him a long time, and I can tell what was done to him on that planet has left scars deeper than those that show on his skin.

"Honored *Tesei*," I address them formally; it's more than they deserve. "We are here for an explanation from you about The Unseen and about the collapse in Haalux birth rate." I raise my voice to ensure that it is heard. "About why you are keeping this information from the Assembly and the Empire. Either of these threats in isolation would warrant a full Assembly, but both place us on a war footing."

"You want more than that though, don't you, Commander? You want to know about your birth and your parents."

"Commander Rexitor is *Istvon*." Bron interjects. "You repressed the research that proved the lineage was still strong, still available. Lineage that will save the Empire."

All around there is the sound of warriors taking in breaths, and I notice there are a number of Assembly members in the chamber. They must have been here before we broke in.

"Commander Rexitor's offspring with his human mate is a disgrace to the Empire." One of the Council members steps forward and pulls off her hood. Dark red eyes of Council member Keela bore into mine. "Never the less," she softens her voice, "we accept that some things have been kept from the Assembly which do pose a threat to the Empire, and it is time to get these into the open."

She turns back to the other hooded Council members who nod their heads.

"We wish to offer you, Rexitor, *Istvon*, a place on the Council. You are a strong warrior and a leader of warriors. We need you to coordinate the fight against the Unseen. Your experience will be invaluable, and as *Istvon*, the populace will follow you. You are needed for your Empire." She says.

I look across at Bron, and he inclines his head, raising his eyebrows. Neither of us expected it to go this well.

"On one condition, *Istvon* Rexitor." Keela holds up a finger, which she slowly moves to point at Jayne. "You rid Haalux of your hybrid mating. Have the child aborted!"

Jayne gasps, placing an arm protectively over her stomach she takes a couple of steps back, just as the chamber door is pried open and the Council guard burst into the room. They are heavily armored. Even with the warriors we have in the chamber, we are outnumbered. One of the guards grabs Jayne, who squeals and jumps, but is unable to get away.

Bron stares at me as one by one, his warriors are surrounded and have blasters pressed at their heads. It only leaves us in the center of the chamber, side by side. I know what I have to do for the good of the Empire and the Haalux species.

"I accept." I look over at Jayne. "Have the child aborted."

"You have chosen wisely, *Istvon*." Keela smiles at me. "Join us."

And I step forward through the hidden door that will take me to the balcony and to the seat of Haalux power.

53

JAYNE

I stare after Rex, unable to comprehend what he has just said.

Did he really just agree to have his child destroyed in order to gain power? I feel my legs sagging, and I would have hit the floor if the big Haalux holding me would let go.

"Bron?" I find my voice and call across the chamber. "Bron? What's happening?" I crack on the final word, and it comes out as a squeak.

"I'm sorry, sweetness," he calls back. "It had to be this way. The *Istvon* will ensure you are treated well for your service." He motions to his men, who drop their weapons, followed slowly by the rest of the new Haalux warriors who just entered the chamber.

"You are to come with me, Jayne." A familiar voice in my ear, and over my shoulder, Jaal steps into view. He's dressed formally, a long silver coat, similar to a doctor's lab coat on Earth, a hypo syringe in one hand. He moves in close, lifting my hair away from my neck in order to get the syringe in. I feel a tiny pinprick as the drug is delivered, and he wavers in my vision as I fall and never hit the ground.

It's all quiet around me as I swim back into consciousness. I'm lying on something comfortable and can feel the weight of a Haalux blanket over me. My hand moves as quickly as I can muster to my stomach. It's still rounded. I risk opening an eye. I'm in a med-pod and across the room, Jaal has his back to me. The weight of Rex's behavior returns to roost in my head. Immediately I'm half paralysed, gasping for breath at the enormity of his betrayal.

"Hey, hey," Jaal is beside me, and I find enough strength to push myself to the other side of the pod.

"Stay away from me and my baby! You're not killing her, you monster!" I spit at him. "What sort of fucking species are you that kills unborn babies because they don't suit your needs? Fuck you!"

I'm, fortunately, fully dressed, including my boots, and I reach for the dagger that Rex gave me, when he— The grief is crippling. I just want to close my eyes, descend into the darkness and never wake up. My hand closes around the shaft and I pull it out, shoving the blade in Jaal's face.

"Back off, Jaal!" I snarl. He immediately scrambles away, his red eyes focussed on the blade. "I should have known you Haalux are all the same. It's all for the Empire. I've no idea why you even have a concept of fated mates."

I climb out of the other side of the pod. My belly still feels full, and I don't think anything has been done to me. If I can get away, the planet is surely big enough for me to find somewhere to hide to have my baby then work out away off this terrible place, where the merest hint of power has a male abandoning his child.

"Jayne-" Jaal calls out.

"Shut it, Jaal!" I look around to see if there is any where I can put the medic so he can't raise the alarm. "What's in there?" I ask nodding at the room behind him.

"It's used for operations." Jaal answers. "Where did you get that dagger?" I notice his eyes still haven't left it.

"It doesn't matter." My breath hitches in my chest. "Get in there!" I flash the blade at him, and he backs away, through the door. "Close it!" I shout at him.

"But-" He protests.

"For fuck's sake! Just do it, Jaal!" I scream at him.

He huffs and presses the panel to close the door. "There's something you need to—" His words are cut off by the closing door.

I stab the knife into the panel on my side, hoping that it's enough to disable the mechanism. The blade slices through the metal like butter, and I hear a satisfying crunch, which is always a sign of something breaking. I've still only got this one blade, and I look around the med-bay for other possible weapons. There's Jaal's hypo-syringe, which I pocket and some ration blocks which I cram into my mouth. I hadn't realized how hungry I was.

A soft chitter grabs my attention and Fitz creeps out from under the pod. He's looking slimmer than normal and appears to be limping. He disappeared when the fire fight started outside, and I thought he had the good sense to find somewhere to hide whilst it was all going on. I cross the room and pick him up. He lets out a sound somewhere between a whimper and a hiss.

"It's okay, Fitz," I stroke his stubby head and he croons. "We'll get out of here and it'll be okay."

I knew I was better on my own. I let the fact that someone took an interest in me blind me to that fact. A mistake I've made before, and it's one I swore not to repeat. Rex has beaten me with my own past, and I hate him for it. This time, I'm going to believe in myself.

Buttoning up my coat, I tuck Fitz inside where he curls up and I shove the remainder of the ration blocks in my other pocket. I approach the door and press the panel to open it. There's no one in the corridor outside, which I wasn't expecting, but then I suppose they probably thought that a drugged, pregnant female was no threat. A sound further up the corridor reminds me I'm not alone in this place and I need to get moving. Creeping out of the med-bay, I head off in the opposite direction to the sound I heard. I know that my knife isn't going to cut it against those heavily armed Haalux that entered the chamber just before Rex betrayed me.

Just the thought of his name has my stomach contracting with anger and pain. It's nothing compared to the stabbing in my heart. I need to concentrate, and I grip the dagger handle as I move as swiftly and as quietly as I can. I see light ahead and all at once, I'm out in the atrium. It's still strewn with evidence of our earlier entrance.

"Going somewhere, female?"

I freeze at the sound of the voice behind me. It's not too far to the outer door, and I wonder if I can outrun a male. Turning, I see the massive Haalux warrior from earlier leaning nonchalantly on a pillar, a blaster pointed at me, his red eyes glittering with menace.

54

REX

A platform lifts me and the Three into the higher echelons of the chamber. When we reach the balcony, the Council move across it and through a door at the end. I find myself in an enormous room situated, it seems, in its own spire. It is furnished sumptuously with items from across the Empire. The fabled Council inner sanctum.

"You made a wise decision, Rexitor." Keela says. "A Haalux *Istvon* cannot be seen to have hybrid children."

One of the other council member has removed his hood. "A hybrid can only pollute the genetic makeup we have striven for these last hundred turns," Council member Irax adds.

"And yet, our genetic meddling has been the death of our species," I reply.

"You know the value of our Empire, Rexitor. You understand it enough to do the right thing." Keela pours herself an amber drink from a Doxian crystal decanter. It's jeweled surface shimmers in the light. "Or you would not have agreed to the destruction of your child."

"I understand the power of the Empire only too well, and it's more than this Council." I say, concentrating on the one Council member still hooded.

"We have scientists working on the procreation problem, Rexitor. They are close to a breakthrough," Irax says. "But we feel that an *Istvon* on the Council will inspire confidence in the populace that the problem is easily surmountable, an injection of old blood. Your seed can father the next generation."

"My next Zycle is not for five turns," I address the hooded figure. "How would that work?"

"Your Zycle has been advanced by the presence of the human female. You can and will be able to seed Haalux females." Keela swallows the remainder of her drink. "You will be able to start straight away. We already have some suitable candidates ready for you."

"It seems you have it all worked out." I smile at Keela who returns my facial expression with some effort.

"We are the Council of Three. Of course we have."

"Except I have not heard from Mejin. What is his opinion? And what do you propose to do about The Unseen?"

"The Unseen are not a threat." A low voice comes from under the hood.

I cock my head to one side. "That's not what I've heard. They were behind the attack on the *Excelsior* and have attempted to infiltrate the heart of the Assembly."

"For what purpose?" Irax asks.

"The same purpose of any enemy of the Empire, to bring us down, only this time from within. Using our society against us, a society that denies its past and puts all of its faith in genetic modifications." I don't take my eyes off the hooded councillor, my hand on the blaster tucked in the waistband at my back.

Keela laughs harshly. "You underestimate the Council and the Assembly, Rexitor, in your rush to become *Istvon*."

"I have no desire to be *Istvon*. All I ever wanted was to serve the Empire, which did its best to crush me at every turn."

"Pathetic," Irax spits. "Why did you ever think he could do this?"

He snarls at Keela, "he's nothing but a miserable child, crying for his mama. He's no leader."

I take this as my cue and pull out the blaster, holding it on Mejin. "Presumably recruiting me was your idea? At least once you found out I was returning to Haalux?"

"How did you know that?" Keela asks, frowning.

"Exactly when did you last see, Councillor Mejin?" I reply to her.

"He's here. And now you are just testing our patience, Rexitor. Are you going to accept the position on the Council or not?"

"Take off your hood," I growl at Mejin. "Take it off, or I will." I step towards Mejin. He takes a step back, then reaches up, slowly pulling the fabric back.

Keela lets out a gasp at what is revealed. Under the hood is a transparent being that is definitely not Haalux. For a second the skull-like head with dead black eyes flickers, and the face of Mejin appears, then it is gone again.

"Get the guard in here!" Irax yells. "Where is Councillor Mejin?" He fires at the being.

"He's long gone, isn't he?" I approach the creature that is masquerading as Mejin. Its features don't change, and it doesn't back away from me, instead holding its ground. The Unseen lets out a harsh metallic laugh that is at once familiar and grating.

"You have no idea how long." The Unseen continues to laugh. "All this time and the only Haalux that got close to the truth was you, Commander. Ambassador Roi intended to seek you out as you were the last to see Mejin alive when you returned his son. That you found your fated mate in the stupid creature set up with his murder was just a bonus."

"It was Mejin who suggested repressing the research into the old genetic line," Keela says quietly. "It seemed logical at the time, before we found out about the birthrate."

"And I bet The Unseen have something to do with that too," I say.

"That we only had to give a little nudge. You were already well on your way to your own destruction. The only good Haalux is a dead Haalux." The Unseen says with a flash in its dead eye sockets. "Same goes for your hybrid, Commander. That too should be long gone by now. Dumped in your quest for power."

I level my blaster at what passes for the thing's head. It grins its permanent abhorrent grin. My vision darkens as I realise what it wanted to do to Haalux and what it wanted me to do in the quest to destroy the Empire. It would have let me kill my own child and destroy my mating bond, had I even considered that option for a second.

"I'm not a leader. I'm not *Istvon*. I'm none of those things. I'm an outcast and that means I get to do the Empire's dirty work, even when it's not wanted."

As I pull the trigger, I'm dimly aware of the shouts of the other Council members. The Unseen's head is ripped apart by the close quarter blast, and its robe crumples to the floor, just as the Council guard burst into the inner sanctum.

"Drop it, Rex." It's Bron. He approaches me carefully, reaching out for the blaster as I stare at what remains of The Unseen. "It's over."

I blink at him as I come to my senses and drop the blaster into his outstretched hand. He heaves a visible sigh of relief.

"Where's Jayne?" It's the only question I want an answer to.

Bron hesitates, "General Kylar has her in the atrium."

"Fuck! She was supposed to be with Jaal!" I make a grab for my blaster, and Bron holds it away from me.

"It's the General, Rex. He'll take more convincing than anyone of the Council's betrayal. You have to be careful!" Bron says in anguish as I snatch the blaster from him and start running for the door.

55

JAYNE

"Did you decide that one murder wasn't enough?" The warrior stares at me with an intensity that actually makes me want to look away.

Unlike the other warriors I have seen, he's dressed in a form fitting suit that is heavily armored. It's so matte black it's almost sucking in the light. He has two crossed swords on his back, although it's the sleek looking blaster in his hand that is taking most of my attention. His lip curls in a snarl as he contemplates me, his angular face emphasizing his single deep electric blue Hallan. His desire to dominate and intimidate is obvious and working.

"I didn't murder anyone." I reply, fingering the knife in my pocket and wondering if its sharp enough to pierce his armor. "I proved that at the trial."

The big Haalux snorts. "Nothing was proven. You used the trial as a smokescreen to allow the Grolix to attack a Haalux warship." His eyes flicker momentarily with emotion that is verging on crazy and then return to their deep red color.

I pull out the knife and try to look as if I know what to do with it.

"So, you're not a murderer? What are you doing with a tilon blade?" He inclines his head, and without moving a muscle, he lets off a blaster blot that blows the dagger out of my hand with a sharp intense heat that has my hand burning in agony.

"I was given it to defend myself from twats like you!" I shout at him as I tuck my smarting hand under my arm in an attempt to reduce the pain.

"By your traitorous mate? Figures." The warrior sneers at me.

He's not going to be won over by anything I say, that much is clear. The way he holds himself and the color of his eyes indicated he's not a grunt. He has rank and experience. He's military through and through. I already know just how hard it was to break through Rex's training. This warrior is older, meaner and has already made up his mind.

"Go on then. Kill a pregnant female," I smooth my hands over my swelling belly. "It's for the good of the Empire after all. Don't bother to ask the question as to why we would come to Haalux unless there was a damn good reason or why a primitive species like mine would dare to challenge the Empire. Shoot first and fuck the consequences!"

"Good of you to make the decision for me," He snarls, leveling the blaster at my head and squeezing the trigger.

Fitz emerges from my coat, a ball of black spitting electricity as the warrior releases the blaster bolt. Out of nowhere, Rex barrels into him and the pair of them go sprawling over the floor of the atrium, debris spinning away from their bodies. He manages to wrestle the blaster from the older warrior and flings it away from them both. But that's not enough. With a roar that seemingly shakes the floor, the warrior leaps onto Rex, aiming punches at his head. They are evenly matched but the way the other warrior fights is cold and calculated. Rex manages to roll out of the way and get to his feet, only to be toppled as the warrior gets in a punch at his abdomen and swipes his legs from under him.

"Jayne, are you okay?" Bron crouches next to me.

"Bron!" I try to scoot away from him.

"Hey, sweetness. You're safe. Your baby is safe. We had to pretend to the Council that Rex would do anything to get power in order to flush out The Unseen," Bron says quietly.

"But why? Why not tell me?" I stumble over my words, trying to take in what he is saying.

"It had to be real. Your reaction had to be real."

"No." I shake my head. "If he cared for me, he would tell me."

"He did it because you're his world. He would do anything to keep you safe and to protect your child." Bron is beside me, one hand on my stomach. "Even if that meant denying everything he has ever wanted. You had to trust him."

"Please stop them fighting, Bron." I whisper, my eyes full of tears I can't control. I don't know what to feel or what to think any more. All I know is that the fight can't go on. I can't bear it any longer.

Bron looks over at Jak, who fires a round over the two Haalux, locked in a wrestling match on the floor. The older is the first to disengage.

It's only then I spot Fitz. He's lying on the ground unmoving. He must have been hit by the blaster bolt. I scramble over to him, and he chuckles quietly as I run my hand over his fur. He's struggling to hold his form, flickering with weak electricity and his invisibility flowing like waves.

'Fitz," I whisper as I gently cup his snub head, "don't leave me. Stay, there's a good Masca. Please stay."

He manages to lift his head as he looks at me, his red eyes glassy with pain and a little blue tongue swipes at my hand. He lets out a muffled purr, then his head drops back to the ground. He lets out a long sigh as he slowly fades away until there is nothing left of him.

56

REX

The General releases me at the sound of the blaster bolt over our heads. I'd still have taken him, even if he wasn't distracted. He spots the numerous blasters pointed at him and makes the sensible choice to surrender. Although if his reputation is anything to go by, it won't be for long.

I search the atrium for Jayne, hoping that I got to her in time. I see her crouched on the ground and within seconds, I've sprinted to her side. The Masca's lithe little form is stretched out on the floor. She whispers to him, and he disappears.

Jayne stares at the place he was, her shoulders heaving as she sobs silently. Finally, she turns in my direction.

"He took the blaster bolt for me." She shudders through her tears.

"Forat said they make loyal pets." I go to put my arm around her. She shrugs me off violently and scrambles to her feet.

"Leave me alone! You don't have a say in what he was!" She shouts at me and runs for the door.

"Jayne!" I go to run after her and feel a heavy hand on my shoulder.

I grab at the hand, intending to twist free, but it's like iron. I look into the hard, red eyes of the General.

"Leave the female. You've some explaining to do, Commander."

Bron is just over his shoulder, arms crossed. He inclines his head at me, looking around at the mess we've made of the Council building. I swing my gaze between him, and Jayne's retreating form. It looks like the *Istvon*'s work is never done.

It seems to take forever to provide the Assembly, the General, his senior staff and the Council guard with the necessary recordings and evidence to show the threat to the Empire, and that it wasn't me, Jayne, or anyone associated with us. Forat's advice to wear a recording eye-lens was invaluable, and the recording of what went on in the Council chamber proved invaluable.

Once the assembly had seen that Mejin was not Haalux and had heard from him, there was a unanimous decision from them that, despite our unorthodox methods, we were right to have taken the emergency action we had without going through the proper channels.

"She's still outside," Jaal says as we finally leave the Council chamber, leaving the Assembly noisily arguing amongst themselves. "I've checked her over and other than a small blaster burn to her hand. She is fine, as is your child."

"Not sure I can say the same about the mating bond." I mutter as I make my way through the atrium that is steadily being cleared by the guard. I exit through the ruined doors and out into a Haalux evening.

Our twin moons, Lux and Gorn are full and hang low in the sky, illuminated in pinks and blues. Sitting with her back to me on the only remaining bench in the gardens is Jayne. The dying light of the suns catches the fire in her hair, and I stand for a moment, just to look at my beautiful mate and to wonder about our future.

She slowly turns to look at me, her eyes intensely blue. They rake over me and she turns away. I descend the steps into the garden and take a seat next to her, not quite touching.

"I'm sorry. I should have told you the plan." I eventually say. Bron has informed me of her horror at what had happened.

"I should have trusted you." Jayne says, staring down at her hands in her lap. "I should have trusted myself."

"It still wasn't fair. You're my mate and you deserved to know the truth." I reach for her hand, curling my gray fingers around her tiny pink ones. "Being mated doesn't mean you can guess." She doesn't pull away.

"A bond needs work, regardless. Nothing's perfect." Jayne raises her eyes to meet mine. "I tried so hard to be perfect, and all it took to bring me down was to trust in the wrong person. I lost a lifetime for nothing. I don't want that with you, Rex. I want you to be my everything." Her bottom lip trembles. "This is as new to me as it is to you."

I'm unable to help myself, I pull her into me and a warmth spreads through my body as she melts into my embrace.

"You can trust me, my *kedves*. You are the mate I never thought I'd ever be worthy of, clever, brave, and resourceful. I promise to always tell you the truth, to love you and to raise our children to do the same."

I kiss away the tears that run down her cheeks until I reach her lips. She captures me, our tongues entwining as I lose myself in her soft heat. I run my hands over her expanding body, delicious and ripe with my child, and I know she's going to have a hard time not always being pregnant. Because now I have her, I'm not going to let her go.

EPILOGUE
JAYNE

Rex gently rocks the tiny baby in his massive arms. The look of love and wonder on his face gets me every time.

Rose was born three months ago, after I endured a long eleven-month pregnancy. Her birth came just as Rex was announced as *Istvon* and took his rightful place at the head of the Council and Assembly. It's a position he didn't want, but I used my words of persuasion to convince him that power should always be in the hands of those who least want it. If the Empire was to counter the new threat from The Unseen, they needed a leader who was above suspicion.

He's used his position to end the practice of confining males in Zycle. Instead introducing a system where males are able to mix with females whether in Zycle or not. It's greatly increased the number of mated pairings, and in turn, this has given a kick start to reversing the breeding crash. Haalux babies are being conceived again. Rex has also put out a decree that any species with Haalux blood is considered Haalux. It turned out there were already quite a few of them, most virtually indistinguishable from other Haalux.

Rex searched for his parents, but the search was fruitless. If they were still alive, they had long since left the Empire. I catch the sadness in his eyes occasionally when he's looking at Rose. I think he would have wanted them to know him and her.

"When you've quite finished, *Istvon*. I need to get her ready for Jaal, then I've got to get dressed."

I swoop in and pluck the baby from him. Rose giggles deliciously as she stares up at me with her orange eyes. Her skin is gray and she has the same markings as Rex on her tiny chest, but Rex says he can see me in her face.

I'm still collecting her things when there is a chime that announces Jaal.

Rex didn't want Rose to grow up in the Council building, so he had the old *Istvon* palace refurbished. It turned out that it was far better for hosting the various gatherings and banquets that his position demands. Like the one being held tonight to celebrate some Haalux holiday or other.

"Hey, Uncle Jaal," I grin at the medic. "You ready for babysitting duty?"

"I guess that I wasn't your first choice," Jaal replies, "given how little I get to see this one." He takes Rose from me, an indulgent smile on his face.

"Well, Bron and Forat have gone after Hardag, so that didn't leave a lot of options." Rex says to a snort of annoyance from Jaal.

"You would leave as precious a thing as this with that pair?"

"Bron would rather chew his own arm off than spend time with a baby and Forat says he's done his share." I attempt to smooth things over with Jaal.

"She will be perfectly safe with me, anyway." Jaal tickles Rose under the chin, making her gurgle happily. "You don't want to spend time with space pirates do you, sweetness." He coos and Rex stifles a laugh.

Rex didn't want Bron to leave, but the proud Captain wouldn't be dissuaded. I got the impression that there was a score to settle. Rex did, however, arrange a series of missions that would keep General Kylar busy, and a long way from Haalux for a while, much to my relief.

Fitz winds his way around my legs, humming as he stares up at Jaal. "I'm not babysitting that Masca!" Jaal exclaims when he spots him.

"Too bad," Rex is really laughing now. "They come as a pair. Fitz!" He whistles and the Masca swarms around Jaal until he has taken residence on his shoulders.

"What does it take to kill this thing?" He grumbles.

"Not a blaster bolt anyway." I say as I stroke the chittering creature on his head and check on Rose in Jaal's arms again.

Fitz had reappeared several days after the battle, looking thin and unable to produce his usual electrical charges, but alive. I've not let him out of my sight since.

"Are you done?" Rex says to Jaal, "My mate has to get ready." He gives Jaal his best *Istvon* stare, which Jaal ignores.

"I will return in the morning." He sweeps out of our apartment.

"You might have hurt his feelings," I say to Rex.

"I don't care." He scoops me up and carries me towards the bedroom. "I need some time alone with my mate to make the next generation of Haalux." He presses his lips on mine, his Hallan hot against my skin and I know we are definitely going to be late to the party.

———

I hope you enjoyed Taken: Alien Commander's Captive.

If you did, you could always leave me a review :)

I can't leave you wanting more though, can I?

Of course not....

Crave: Alien General's Obsession is the second in the Haalux Empire Series.

———

You can get an alert for all my new releases before anyone else by signing up for my newsletter. As a thank you for subscribing, you get my steamy sci-fi novella 'Angel and the Alien Brute' absolutely free!

You'll also get sneak peaks from my latest work, cover reveals and more.

So if you want all of the above, sign up HERE

If not, that's totally cool too.

You can also follow me on Amazon if you so wish, but I'm always going to say my newsletter is better!

ALSO BY HATTIE JACKS

Rogue Alien Warriors Series

Fierce

Fear

Fire

Fallen

Forever

———

Haalux Empire Series

Taken: Alien Commander's Captive

Crave: Alien General's Obsession

Havoc: Alien Captain's Alliance

Bane: Alien Warrior's Redemption

Traitor: Alien Hunter's Mate

JUST WHO IS THIS HATTIE JACKS ANYWAY?

I've been a passionate sci-fi fan since I was a little girl, brought up on a diet of Douglas Adams, Issac Asimov, Star Trek, Star Wars, Doctor Who, Red Dwarf and The Adventure Game.

What? You don't know about The Adventure Game? It's probably a British thing and dates me horribly! Google it. Even better search for it on YouTube. In my defence, there were only three channels back then.

I'm also a sucker for great characters and situations as well as grand romance, because who doesn't like a grand romantic gesture?

So, when I'm not writing steamy stories about smouldering alien males and women with something to prove, you'll find me battling my garden or zooming around the countryside on my motorbike.

Check out my website at www.hattiejacks.com!

The inspiration for Fitz
So much more than 'just a cat'
Long since passed over the rainbow bridge
I miss you every day, B
The nights you pad into my dreams are the best.

Printed in Great Britain
by Amazon